REAPER'S DELIVERANCE

Reaper's Deliverance

Miranda Stork

Published by Moon Rose Publishing

ISBN-13: 978-1-909816-70-1

REAPER'S DELIVERANCE

*'The blue metal bore down on him,
and he braced himself for the impact,
willing his body to survive, even
though he knew it was too late.'*

CHAPTER ONE

The lights blinded him as the loud truck horn sounded into the night, warning him of his imminent death, but it was too late. Ryder screamed and threw his arms up as though to protect himself, the vibration of the bike throbbing through his body like his heartbeat, and he braced himself for the crash. It was too late. It was going to kill him. *It's all too late. I'm going to die.*

It was a night like any other for his gang. Drinking, smashing bars up, running from the cops. It was what they did for fun. And the fact it was New Year's only sweetened the deal. Free-flowing alcohol, girls dancing with very little inhibitions, and loud music. It was paradise.

Gilbert Ryder Thompson looked up from the bar towards the swaying mass of bodies writhing against each other, grinding and shifting to the thump of the bass. The music rang in his ears, filling them and sending his pulse into the same rhythm, a heavy dance track that begged for movement against strangers. The singer crooned something about '*love forever*' as the bass kicked up a notch, driving like a tribal drum. Ryder snorted as he raised the glass of bourbon to his lips. *Love forever. Give me a break.*

The nightclub was lit up with blinking fluorescents, casting every colour across the sweating faces of the dancers. He leaned back against the polished bar surface behind, a slab of speckled grey marble coated in sticky residue from knocked over drinks, taking an large sip of the amber liquid in his hand. Ryder might have been a thug, but he could appreciate the finer forms of alcohol. *Like father, like son, I guess. Like mum, too.* His fingers tightened against the thin glass at the thought of his parents, the skin turning white as he gripped it harder. The sip became a draught, and he finished off the drink with a smack of his lips, slamming the glass down onto the bar. The bartender gave him a raised eyebrow, but said nothing before racing over to serve someone at the other end.

A woman caught Ryder's eye, lost somewhere in the middle of the crowd. She was gyrating wildly against her friend, her long blond hair falling across her shoulders in clumped strands, her mini-skirt riding up her arse as she swivelled her hips. A long ladder had stretched down the back of her tights, but she didn't seem to care much about her appearance as she held her hands in the air with the beat turning up, a bottle of cheap alcopop in one palm. Ryder gave a satisfied grunt as he watched the woman twisting to the music, shifting his hips against the tight, ripped jeans he wore, his eyes travelling down her form. His crotch twitched in response to his thoughts, and he ran a slow tongue across his lips. *Drunk, barely dressed, and hot. Just how I like 'em.* To his delight, the woman looked up for a moment towards him and caught his eye, biting her lip at his figure. Ryder's lips curved into a confident grin, and he tilted his chin back, making it clear he was watching her.

He knew he looked good tonight. Hell, he looked good every night. If there was one thing he had learned about a certain kind of woman, it was that they rocked the bad boy look, and they didn't care if you were a bastard beneath it. Hair dyed dark blue and twisted into a modern quiff, a close-fitting leather biker jacket over his torso, he stood out in a crowd without having to utter a word. As he stared at the woman, just about ready to nod her across, she collapsed to the dancefloor as she tripped over her own feet. Giggling hysterically, she teetered herself upright as her friend helped her up again, managing to keep the bottle of alcohol carefully balanced in her outstretched hand. Ryder raised his eyebrows and swiftly turned around, striding further into the darkness of the club. *I like drunk, but not that drunk. She'd throw up on me before we even got to taking her lack-of-bra off.*

Letting out a troubled sigh, he glanced over towards one of the others in their gang, a young guy called Matthew. He was only eighteen, but he had already been inside on more charges than any of them had eaten hot meals. Robbery, GBH, a string of assaults…Ryder didn't really like the guy, but he was a good laugh, when he was in the right mood. The lad was busying fawning over a woman propped against the end of the bar. She was staring at him in a bored fashion, more interested in the music than him, judging by how she kept twisting around to the music and staring over his shoulder. Shaking his head, Ryder chuckled to himself at the lad's persistence, not giving up as she tried in vain to give him the elbow.

Ryder's jacket creaked as he moved away from the bar with a graceful push, striding over towards Matthew and the poor woman he had trapped in his unrequited sights. Raising his voice above the ear-splitting noise, Ryder tapped the young man on his worn blue Adidas hoodie, and shouted, "Leave it, mate! She's not interested. Get someone else." He gestured with a thumb over his shoulder towards the waiting myriad of people on the thumping dancefloor, giving an apologetic nod to the woman. She said nothing, carrying on with her dancing, but she gave him an appraising look from head to toe with her mascara-blurred eyes.

Matthew, in his typical fashion, shoved Ryder's arm away with a toss of his hand. He staggered forwards, the ten beers he had downed earlier in the evening finally kicking in. Jabbing a finger in Ryder's face, his eyelids lowered in an alcoholic haze, he slurred, "Now…now…listen, mate. I like you…er, Ryder. But I'm trying to chat this bird up, so keep your…fucking face out, right?" Nodding vigorously as though he had said the wisest words ever spoken by man, he twisted on his heel and turned his attention back to the bored brunette.

Rolling his shoulders as he heaved a sigh, Ryder was about to try dragging him away again, when he saw a six-foot man making a beeline for Matthew and the women, his face contorted with rage. *Fuck. Shit's about to get real.* The tall man, dressed in a sporty t-shirt and gold chain with a shaved head, raced over and snatched the woman's arm up in his grasp, yanking her to his side. She giggled, leaning up and pecking him on the cheek, gazing slyly back over to Matthew. The kiss had no effect, as her boyfriend continued staring down the short eighteen-year-old. "You trying to come on to my woman?"

Smelling the tension building before he even reacted, Ryder gripped Matthew's shoulders tightly, despite his struggles. Pulling him back, he smiled easily, and yelled back, "Sorry, mate. He's had too much, you know what kids are like!" As if to add emphasis to his point, he raised his lean hand and made swirling motions against his temple, shaking his head from side to side. His icy blue eyes bore into the man's face with cold indifference, telling him silently to step back.

"I'm not a fucking kid!" Matthew protested, shrugging himself free of his comrade's grasp, sizing up to the taller man. Swaying as he planted his feet, he fisted his hands by his sides and sneered, "Yeah, I was coming onto her. What the fuck you going to do about it?"

The shaven-headed guy pushed his girlfriend behind him, where she tutted and tossed her hair over her shoulder, as though this was a normal practice every night. Face turning bright red, he snatched up the front of Matthew's shirt, snarling, "You little shit!"

Quick as lightning, the mouthy teenager pulled his head far back, waited a second to take in the sight of the bigger man's mouth dropping in shock, and smacked his forehead into the bridge of the guy's nose. Ryder put a hand to his head and squeezed his temples, groaning as he silently cursed Matthew for being in the same bar as him that night. He was an idiot for starting fights over nothing. The boyfriend's grip loosened as he reeled backwards, landing hard on the wooden floor as he howled and clutched at his nose. His girlfriend gave a shriek, shuffling backwards on her teetering heels, her hands flying to her mouth as the first blood trickled from her partner's nostrils. The crowd shambled back in one movement, clearing the space around Matthew and the taller man, whispers and gasps of horror going up from them in a collective voice. The music carried on from the speakers with a vengeance, the lights flashing across the fight, as though urging them on.

Just when I wanted one New Year's without getting in a fight. I'm getting too old for this shit. The taller guy rose up, wiping the back of his hand across his nose and staring down at the resulting red stain with revulsion in his eyes, before lurching forwards with his fists sailing through the air at Matthew. Thinking quickly, Ryder reached to his side and picked the nearby bar stool up in one hand, gripping the cool steel of the leg while narrowing his eyes. *I don't want to kill the guy, after all. Aim to knock him cold, nothing more.* Shoving Matthew out of the way, Ryder arced his arm and brought the wooden seat of the stool crashing onto the crown of the man's skull.

For a second, the man barely swayed, staring over at Ryder with accusatory eyes, his features drawn back with surprise. He fell like a sack of potatoes to the floor, his head lolling back and forth as he blacked out with a soft groan. Three men pushed their way to the front of the crowd gathered around the scene, all gaping down at the fallen man with growing fury, clenching their fists tightly. Matthew gave a snide laugh, jutting his chin in their direction. Waving his finger towards the bleeding man, he called out, "Friend of yours, I'm guessing?"

Without waiting for a response, the young thug charged across, planting a well-aimed punch to one of the men, smack in his guts. Just before Ryder ran up behind him, he was tapped on the shoulder by a heavy hand. Twisting around with fists raised, he breathed out with relief as he came face to face with Greg and at least five others of their gang. Greg had been Ryder's blood-brother since they were smoking at the bottom of the school field. An argument over the same girl, one scuffle, and they were firm friends from the moment they made up. They were the first two in their 'gang', getting in and out of trouble together, before they recruited other members. They hadn't meant for it to become such a big group, but there seemed to be a lot of guys in their town that liked getting into trouble too. Greg's bearded face and bright red mohican was a surprisingly soothing sight while dealing with the idiotic fury of Matthew, and Ryder felt his shoulders relax. Nodding towards the scene with shining brown eyes, a wide smile spread over Greg's face as he shouted, "Can't take you lot anywhere. Shall we?"

Giving a sharp nod with a grin, Ryder sprinted

across the sticky wooden floor, his pulse racing in time with the monotonous, thudding beat of music that vibrated through the ground. Flashes of light danced in front of his eyes as though he were having an epileptic fit, distracting him for a few seconds as he threw his closed fist into the pile of men that tumbled in the cleared space. His hand connected with soft flesh, and he felt the burn of the punch zipping through his knuckles. Bringing his hand back again, he blinked against the dart of orange light from the fluorescents and threw his weight behind it, launching it into the eye socket of one of the fallen man's friends. Cries and shouts rose up above the music, making his head spin with the noise buzzing through his mind, swirling with the earlier bourbon in a cacophony of sensations. The men fell under the rhythmic assault from the gang, blood mixing with the alcopops spilt on the laminate flooring as seconds ticked by.

Two strong arms gripped Ryder around his torso as he was mid-kick, and he pulled away from the groaning victims on the ground, spinning around to land his fist on the bulb of Greg's nose. Eyes widening, he clutched his friend as he staggered backwards, yelling, "Didn't see you there, mate!"

"No, clearly!" Greg cried back, rubbing his nose with one hand, beckoning frantically with his other. His tall mohican bounced as he jerked his head towards the exit, adding, "Someone's called the coppers. We've got to get out of here, now!"

Leaving the four men slumped on the ground, Ryder and the other seven of his comrades fought their way through the crowd, drinks splashing on them as people's arms were jogged. Several of the women let out screams and pulled away, tripping on their heels and sinking backwards into their friends as they tried to keep out of the way. Ryder shoved past them all with rough hands, the need to get of the club driving his limbs as he sprinted towards the dark exit.

Knocking a young couple out of the way as he barged outside, the scent of overcooked burgers and stale beer rushing into his nostrils, he took a frantic second to take in his surroundings and centre himself in the cold reality of outside. One of the bouncers by the doorway leaned in towards him, but he grabbed the man's lapels before he could speak, smacking his head into the bouncer's sunglasses. The guy staggered back, crashing into the brick wall behind as his shades came off in two pieces on the pavement. Ryder heard shouts from over his shoulder as some of his friends dealt with the other bouncer, pumping his arms so hard the adrenaline took over the throbbing against his forehead, skirting the building around the corner.

The others had arrived in their cars, but Ryder had arrived in style, on his pride and joy. A gleaming Ducati Supersport sat at the edge of the carpark, polished up in slick black paint with flashes of glinting steel. As the others thundered along the pavement behind him, the fresh night air soaking under his thin t-shirt and sending shivers up his arms, Ryder raced across and leapt onto the bike. Greg and Matthew shouted something to him in unison as he revved up the powerful engine, their voices lost over the growl of the bike. He shook his head, giving a panicked shrug as he kicked the bike-stand up with a practised move, growling to himself in exasperation as they continued yelling before jumping in their cars. *What the hell are they saying? I can't hear a fucking thing.* His ears still rang with the level of noise they had been subjected to that night, disorientating him with the combination of alcohol and his headbutt on the bouncer. Stomach twisting as though he was going to throw up, he swallowed it back hard and turned glacier-blue eyes out towards the road.

The wail of sirens filled the air, followed by the screech of tyres somewhere on the other side of the nightclub. The thump of dizzying music still pounded out from the club, matching Ryder's heart as it hammered against his ribs. Not waiting to see if the others were following him, he twisted the handles towards the main road through the town, and hit the accelerator, lurching forwards as the heavy clatter of police feet came behind him. Ignoring the shouts and yells, he pulled out onto the road and sped onwards, picking up speed as he pressed his foot harder.

He grinned broadly as the wind he kicked up breezed under the neck of his jacket, sending a rush of cold air tingling down his spine. He narrowed his eyes as he zipped around corners and roundabouts, dipping and diving as though he was on a racecourse. Horns and shouts came and went in isolated blocks of sound as he passed streets full of taxis and club-goers, and he skidded around a red vehicle as it halted in time from an adjoining road. Blood raced through his veins at the thrill, and Ryder let out a joyous laugh, tilting his head back as he became a blur against the muted colours of the quiet neighbourhoods he passed through.

A siren cut through his senses, a mournful wail fast catching up on his tail. Gritting his teeth, Ryder drove the bike harder, gliding around cars as he weaved through the late night traffic. *Not again. I'm not fucking going back in, I've only been out six months.* Sweat formed on his forehead as he felt the throttle of the beast under his legs vibrating across his skin, freezing like ice as it was whipped by the wind. He couldn't go back inside. Not after the last time. If it was a choice between prison and getting injured, he would risk injury. There were a lot of people in jail he had pissed off over the years, and he would rather not meet them again if he could help it. Coming to the end of the main roadway, Ryder dared a glance over his shoulder, red and blue flashes filling his vision as the police cars narrowed the distance between him and themselves.

He pulled his head back to the road, confusion flooding his brain as he was met with the grill of a large blue truck. A cry of terror ripped itself from his throat as the horn blared loudly into the night, warning him of his impending doom. The headlights of the massive vehicle flashed on and off, blinding him, and he couldn't stop himself from throwing an arm up to shield his eyes. *The bike's going too fast. The bike's going too fast. I'll never stop in time.* Ryder slammed the brake down, but the bike squealed with protest as it was forced down sharply from the breakneck speed he had been travelling at. The blue metal bore down on him, and he braced himself for the impact, willing his body to survive, even though he knew it was too late. There was a grinding slam as metal twisted into metal, and the air was knocked from his body as he hit the truck at full speed, feeling as though his lungs had sprung out from his throat. The world tornadoed around him, colours and sounds whirling together in a maelstrom as the bike twisted out from under his legs, throwing Ryder to the ground.

As Ryder Thompson hit the cold, hard ground beneath his cheek, grit digging into his flesh, a burning sensation ripped across his legs and torso, and he gave a gurgle as he tried to cry out, red liquid pooling across his vision. Blinking a few times as the world darkened, he clutched at the air weakly as booted feet charged across to him, blue and red flashing lights meeting his gaze. He tried to move his other arm, but it wouldn't move when he willed it to, leaving only a cold throbbing as he twitched his shoulder. Voices cried out above him, but they were far away and underwater, burbling in non-coherent syllables as he tried to respond. His tongue was thick against his mouth, and the air grew thinner as he gulped for it, closing his eyelids against the brilliant lights as he gave into the heavy throb behind them...

CHAPTER TWO

Damn, my head feels like someone split it against a wall. Ryder let out a groan, keeping his eyes closed against the dancing sparks of light behind his eyelids as he reached a hand up to his forehead. The throbbing from the collision was still present, but it had dulled into a numb ache, leaving his limbs sore and bruised. Rolling over onto his elbows, he gritted his teeth as he eased himself up into a sitting position, fire racing along the torn sinews of his legs. *I must have hit that truck hard. But I've survived, somehow. Wait...shouldn't I be in a hospital?*

Ryder had been in hospital enough from stab wounds and motorbike accidents to know what one looked like. And the cold, hard surface beneath his outstretched palms didn't feel like a hospital bed. Cracking his eyes open, hissing as stabbing pain hit his temples with the movement, he blinked a few times and stared down at his hands. Black marble met his sight, speckled with white bubbles and pockets of prehistoric air. "What the...?" he murmured to himself, chest clenching with panic. Pushing himself up as he ignored the ache in his arms, he rose up, gazing around as his jaw dropped. His blood froze to ice as he took in his surroundings, pulling his thick leather jacket tighter around his chest.

It didn't look like any hospital he'd ever been in. Ryder stood at the centre of a grandiose hall, covered floor to ceiling in more of the elegant black marble, each polished surface gleaming softly in the gentle glow of candles in silver holders along each wall. Great arches of the stonework pushed the ceiling so far above that it made him dizzy to tilt his head back and stare up at it. The ceiling itself was a velvety, dark blue, that looked as though it was covered in a million twinkling stars. The sight was both empowering and ominous at once. Breathing hard, Ryder twisted around, dread gripping his heart as he searched for the way out. "Hello? Is anyone there?"

A noise from the far end made him swivel around in alarm, his heart thumping against his ribs with so much force he was sure they would break. Pursing his lips up in a fierce snarl, he glanced up towards the distant end of the hall, clenching his hands into tight, sweaty fists. Perspiration prickled at his forehead again as he realised this was somewhere far stranger than a hospital. Narrowing his eyes, he muttered, "It can't be..."

Two immense thrones were perched alone on a raised platform of steps, skulls lining either side. On the larger throne sat a figure in a long black cloak, his features obscured by the draped hood he wore over his head. Pale hands could be made out from his wide sleeves, one of them gripping a tall staff of dark wood. The figure beside him was a woman, with long, black curling hair and skin like ice. Her red eyes silently bored into Ryder, three crows hopping between the shoulders of her feathered dress, shimmering with oily blue and green hues as she shifted.

The cloaked figure steadily got to his feet, the clap of his staff against the marble echoing across the wide arches above their heads. He stepped forwards before descending the steps with care, lifting one deathly white hand and crooking a finger. Ryder had no doubt the cloaked man was beckoning to him, and fear began a slow build in the pit of his stomach. The female beside him stood up gracefully, coming to stand behind him as she jutted her chin back, watching Ryder as she smiled thinly with blood-red lips.

This is a joke. A sick joke one of the others is playing on me. Ryder let out a shaking breath, digging his nails into the soft flesh of his palms as he shook his head vigorously. Thoughts tumbled one over the other in his mind, shifting against each other in a flurry of colours and faces. The fear in the pit of his stomach squeezed at him, and he felt the hairs rising up on the back of his neck in response. Limbs trembling, he staggered backwards, away from the nightmare in front of him. The hooded figure simply crooked its finger again, letting out a deep, mournful sigh.

Ryder blew in and out a few calming breaths, drawing himself up and sticking his chin out proudly. *Come on, Ryder, what the fuck are you frightened of? It's a joke.* Making the decision firm in his mind, he swallowed back the bile that threatened to erupt from his throat, striding across the hall confidently. His footsteps echoed sharply back to him, the hard rubber soles of his boots hitting the floor with uncustomary heaviness. Stopping just shy of the two figures, Ryder felt a chill travel along his skin, lifting hairs with it in its wake as he parted his dry lips and passed his tongue across them. "So, who's the joker? Is it Greg? Matthew? It was Matthew, wasn't it?" He let out a dry chuckle, his nerves jumping at the croakiness of his own voice.

When no response came from either of the figures gazing down at him with their dark expressions, anger flared in his gut, his natural reaction to anything being withheld from him. It was a reaction every probation officer and police officer had ever seen from him. Temples throbbing, Ryder glanced from one to the other with wild eyes, screaming, "Tell me who the *fuck it was!*"

"It's no use shouting, young man. I'm stood right in front of you, and I can hear perfectly, despite my age," the cloaked man intoned. His voice boomed across the hall, and the resonance of the tone brought memories of worlds long since passed, of lives come and gone in the blink of an eye. He lowered his crooked arm, the fabric of his cloak whispering as he shifted down the steps to come closer. Ryder lifted his boot as if to take a step back, but held his ground, tensing his jaw. The man paused for a second, holding the staff out for the woman by his side to take. She gripped it silently, grasping the wood with both hands as she brought it before her and rested on it.

The man brought his hands up to the hood, pulling it back deliberately. Ryder bit his tongue to prevent whimpering as the deathly countenance of the figure was revealed. His skin was as pale as snow, both eyes milky-white and blind, no hair on his head. Wrinkles covered his skin, but there was something youthful about the way he held himself. "Gilbert Ryder Thompson, I am sorry to greet you here, for one so young. This," he continued, gesturing around the grand space with raised arms, "is the Hall of Rest."

"What is this? What's going on?" Ryder bit out, taking the step back with his boot as he swallowed hard to coax saliva back into his dry mouth.

The figure fixed him with both milky eyes, and uttered, "My name is Ankou, and this is my wife, Morrigan. We are the Guardians of Death. It is our solemn duty to help those who have died...pass over into their next life."

The words slammed into Ryder like the truck had slammed into his fragile body. Air evaporated from his lungs, and he clutched at his throat, wheezing for oxygen as his insides twisted. Shaking his head vigorously, he teetered back until he thumped into a marble pillar behind, eyes moving from Ankou to Morrigan with terror as he muttered, "This is a joke, it's a fucking joke. I'm losing my mind. Yeah, that's it. The crash put me in a coma, and this is a dream —"

"I'm so sorry, Gilbert. The crash killed you. You have passed on into the Hall of Rest, so that you may begin your new life. Please allow me to explain to you." Ankou glided off the steps and over towards Ryder, holding a hand out in a kindly gesture. His features remained expressionless, but his blind eyes glimmered with emotion.

Ryder leapt away from the pillar with a growl, stabbing his finger in the air towards the cloaked guardian. "N-No one calls me Gilbert, my name is *Ryder!* Y-You fucking stay away from me! Stay a-away, you hear me?" Twisting on his heel, he sprinted over to the other side of the hall, darting from side to side as he searched for a way out. *There has to be a door. This is a set-up, a sick, sick set-up. I'm not dead. There's a door here, and then I'm getting out. I'm not dead. I'M NOT DEAD.*

There was a bang against the marble floor as Morrigan slammed the staff against it, echoing down the hall to Ryder, still racing back and forth between the great arches that rose above his head. Even as he placed his feet on the floor, a force came out of nowhere that clawed him back to the platform of thrones, landing him heavily on his behind and gasping for air. The red-eyed beauty strode down towards him, the crows on her shoulders hopping nervously about, one of them taking off in a graceful flight before landing next to Ryder. He stared down at the creature cocking his head at him with a loud caw, swivelling around and backing away from Morrigan on his hands and knees, muttering incoherently to himself as his head swivelled from side to side.

She caught up to him, grasping his chin tightly and lifting his face to hers. Ryder's glacier eyes widened as he was forced to look into her otherworldly features, sweat breaking out afresh over his skin and sending itches travelling over his body. "Ryder, you must calm down," she whispered. Her voice was surprisingly soothing and calm, softer than her appearance might have led him to believe. From all the women he had come across, she looked as though she might just stab him through the heart and eat it for lunch. The ghost of a smile crept across her stained lips, and she released his chin gently, crouching down to come to eye-level with him. "I know this is a hard thing to accept. We do not relish informing those who have died that their past life is gone. It's not an easy thing to impart. But the longer you run away, the longer until we explain what has happened to you."

Heart still ricocheting between his ribs like a bullet, Ryder passed a look between the two figures, taking in their solemn but understanding expressions. The truth hit him like a punch to the guts, and a lump formed in his throat before he had a chance to stop it. His eyes prickled with tears, and he blinked hard as a few managed to squeeze out onto his cheeks, streaming down until they hit the corners of his mouth. Passing his tongue out to catch the salty water, he tried hard to remember the last thing that passed before he came here. *The truck. Headlights and horn blaring. The coppers behind me. It caught my bike, and I was thrown off. I heard the metal crunching. Then I was on the road, and there was blood. My blood.* The well of grief in his chest coming loose, Ryder let out a mournful cry, rubbing the back of his hand roughly across his eyes to prevent the tears as he sniffled, "I'm fucking d-dead. I d-don't want to be. Please, let me g-go back. I know I did some stuff, but I—"

Ankou came to stand beside his wife, bending down and laying an icy hand on Ryder's shaking shoulder. "It doesn't work that way, young man. We do not get to choose who comes and who goes. There are exceptions, but this is not one of them. Life naturally ends, but we cannot pick when or who. All we can do is aid you in passing over peacefully."

Sniffing loudly, Ryder raised bloodshot eyes to Ankou, wiping his fingers over his streaming nostrils. "So I can't go back?"

"No. I'm sorry."

Flashes of his life filtered through his mind, a dazzling array of all his crimes and the victims he had taunted. *They'll probably be glad to see me gone.* His shoulders slumped as he let the words sink in. *Dead. I'm dead. It's all gone. I wasted my whole life.* As the last of the tears filtered from his soul, Ryder stood up carefully, using his arm to push himself off the ground. Sighing resignedly, he gave a slow nod. "Okay. I guess...I have to accept it. I don't want to, but I remember the truck. I've gone." Running a hand over his dark hair, he croaked, "I wonder if anyone will remember me. Any of the guys."

Morrigan smiled again, a motherly action that lit her features. "They will remember you, young Ryder. You were like a brother to so many of them. But you must leave that life behind now." Pointing with a red nail-tipped hand, she jerked her head towards the side of the hall. "Come. We will see where your next life will take you."

Limbs heavy as though weighed down by sleep, Ryder took in a deep breath and drew himself up. Jutting his chin out cockily, he strode in the direction Morrigan pointed, rubbing at his now sore eyes. *What the hell, Ryder. You've really messed up this time. No going back from this.*

A glowing orange light beckoned from under one of the arches, and Ryder made his way towards it, aware of the rustling behind him as Ankou followed with his sweeping cloak. As he rounded the corner, he was greeted with the sight of a large pool of water, the same black rock walls as the hall, lit up with the soft light of dripping wax candles. The water shimmered and moved of its own accord, a blue mist rising from it with distant voices and singing. The sight was beautiful and ethereal at once, leaving Ryder feeling like no human should ever really see something like it.

The pair of guardians swept past him, making their way to either side of the pool, Ankou beckoning Ryder forwards with a bony finger. Trepidation settling in his frayed nerves, he forced himself to move towards the whispering liquid, one foot in front of the other until he reached the stone edge of it. Bending and passing a hand across the surface of the water, Ankou lifted his wizened face to Ryder and urged, "Please, take a look. It is your next life. You must be prepared for what is to come."

Raising his eyebrows, Ryder craned his neck and stared down into the blue mist. It parted as he gazed downwards, the pool rippling as it shimmered and revealed images to him, each one flickering into life like an old television screen. First there was a small baby with a deformed leg and skull, crying in its cot as it wailed alone for its mother, a mother who wouldn't come when it called for her. It soon learned not to cry, that crying would only result in a drunken burn from a cigarette. Then a small boy, limping on his way to school, where he was bullied by his schoolmates for his disabilities. The same schoolmates, hitting him until his ears bled, kicking him down a flight of stairs when he couldn't run away from their taunts. The boy became a teenager, weak and afraid of the world as he was beaten mercilessly by those he knew as family, crushed by his life and his own thoughts. Used one fateful night by a cruel and unforgiving boy he once called a friend, raped and scarred in his mind. An adult, alone and scared in his apartment at night, crying himself to sleep as he cut himself for relief, contemplating the end. The same adult, older but bitter at the world, abused and spat upon, haunted each night by the torment of his childhood with no one to comfort him.

Ryder's head throbbed from the images, and he clapped a hand to his mouth, shaking his head as he jabbed a shaking finger down at the water. "So...this is what I have to come? But this is worse than the life I just had!"

Morrigan spread her hands out in an apologetic gesture, sighing as she replied, "Ryder, it is your actions in your past life that have shaped your future one. You cannot expect to have a good future when you have mistreated your past so badly."

Grateful at last for the familiar rush of fury that ignited within, Ryder spat out, "I had to live through my parents, through everyone who never gave a shit about me, through being stomped under society's boot, to get *this?*" Growing braver with each word, he nodded knowingly and cast blazing eyes at them both, adding, "Fuck you, and fuck this place. I'm not going. I won't be cast into another life, not after the one I just had. Not if that's what's waiting for me. It's not my fault the cards life dealt me!"

Ankou's milky eyes flickered over the irate form of Ryder, his hands reaching back and pulling the hood of his cloak back over his head as he explained, "No, but it was up to you how you played out those cards, young man. No one forced you to be the bully. No one forced you to take the law into your own hands so often. You made those choices, and never thought about the consequences. I'm sorry, but..." He paused in his speech, glancing over at Morrigan. Her eyes widened as he looked over, an unspoken conversation passing between them in the silence. Turning back to Ryder, he softly added, "There is...one other option. But it's not an easy one."

Grasping onto any straw of hope, Ryder took in a few calming breaths, his chest heaving with the effort. Rolling his shoulders, he bent his head, replying, "Anything. I'll take anything over that."

Ankou glided across, reaching out for his staff as he swept by Morrigan, hesitancy clear in his tone as he said grimly, "You died on the last second of the last hour of the year. This puts you in a unique position, young man. You may become a Reaper."

CHAPTER THREE

"Reaper?" Ryder's tone was incredulous. "As in, grim?"

Morrigan swept across in a volley of feathers, holding her hand out as one of the crows returned to its perch and its mother. Giving a wry smirk, she replied, "As in 'grim', yes, although we don't use that term. It's used by some of our younger reapers as a joke, but certainly not ours by right."

Ankou placed a bony arm around Ryder's shoulders, steering him back towards the Hall of Rest. The peaty scent of autumn leaves and wet soil drifted from him, curling Ryder's nostrils as he glanced up towards the hooded guardian. "You see, young man, we cannot be in all places at once. But souls have to be collected when they pass over." He paused, his long fingers tapping as though he were collecting his thoughts. "You, and others like you, do not get the chance to be brought over peacefully, your passings are too sudden. But for others, we send a reaper to collect them. They help the deceased to come to the Hall of Rest with ease."

Feeling tension under the deep intonation of Ankou's words, Ryder separated himself to twist and stare at him, raising an eyebrow. "And? There's something else, isn't there?"

Ankou cleared his throat, letting out a rich laugh. "You're very astute, Ryder. Yes, there is. We collect the souls so that they will not be taken by another, so that they may go on to their next life instead. It is a reaper's duty to ensure that happens."

"What 'other'?"

Morrigan let out a heavy sigh at Ryder's sharp question, bringing up the rear as they stepped back into the soft brightness of the Hall. Pursing her lips for a second, she answered, "There are other kinds of reapers, ones who work for another realm. They wish to gain the souls to use for their own purposes. It is a battle that has been continuing for millennia, and is unlikely to change." She clapped her hands together abruptly, and the crows separated once more, flying to the high rafters as they let out cries. An orb of black energy appeared between her hands, and she nodded over to Ryder. "So. Will you accept our offer? Or do you wish to move on to your next life?"

"Wait, wait." Ryder held his hands up as though to protect himself from the crackling ball of magic, glancing nervously from one guardian to the other, both watching him with silent stares. "I need to know more about this. Is this forever?"

Leaning weightily on his staff with both hands, Ankou shook his head, the hood flapping back and forth with the movement. "No, only for one-hundred years. After that, you will have paid back your dues for the life you have led, and you can move freely onto a new life, a better life."

"Can I talk to anyone when I…er…collect souls? Can I go and see my friends?"

"No." The answer was a stony as the speaker, Ankou's voice booming across the short distance between them. "You are never to speak to anyone but your fellow reapers, and those you are collecting for the next life. I'm truly sorry, young Ryder. But you can never see your friends or family again."

Ryder snorted at that. *As if I'd want to see my family again.* He chewed at his lip, slowly lowering his arms as he considered his two options. *A hundred years? Long time to flit around collecting people like a paranormal hoover. But my next life...it's worse that my current—last, I guess—life. I can't do it. I always hoped that one day things would get better. If this is my only way to make it happen...I'll do it.*

Having made his decision, Ryder took in a deep breath, nodding over at Morrigan. "Alright, I'll do it. 'Reaper' me."

Before he had a chance to blink, Morrigan bent and threw the ball of energy towards him, enveloping him in its dark mist. It crackled and swirled around him, lifting him gently from the floor as though he weighed nothing. Ryder let out a sharp cry as he was raised from the ground, holding his arms out to keep his balance. The energy spun him around, faster and faster as it took hold. It stuck to his skin, sending a thrill through him as he felt it sinking into his body, expanding and fitting to its form in his soul. There was a searing pain through his right arm, and he glanced down towards it, yanking his leather sleeve back hurriedly. A long line of black fire hissed its way along his skin, leaving a smoking tattoo in its place, a winding trail of flames crowned by a single skull.

As the magic drifted into mist, lowering him carefully back onto his own two feet once more, Ryder continued staring down at the tattoo with wide eyes, a grin breaking across his lips. "Hey, this is pretty cool."

Morrigan's lips twitched at the remark, and she gestured up above the thrones, towards a large stone engraving etched into the wall. It was the same tattoo on Ryder's arm, a curling trail of fire crowned by a single grinning skull. "It is the symbol of all reapers. It reminds us of the fragility of life and your duty. And the fire reminds us of the spark of rebirth and new life. Wear it with pride, Ryder."

Ryder stared up towards the image on the wall, drinking it in as his cool gaze swept across it. A chill trickled down his back as he thought about what he was now a part of. A Reaper. A chance to make up for the shit in his life. A new beginning.

"This is the Catcher. Don't you dare go near it unless you're supposed to. I swear, I don't need another lecture from Ankou about Reapers coming through with beer. Hell, no." The theatrical man in front of Ryder waved his hands in mock despair, rolling his dark brown eyes with a loud sigh of exasperation.

'Greek, as he had been introduced to Ryder — not, he proclaimed, because he preferred Greek men, but merely because of his own Grecian god-like looks — was apparently the man to speak to if you were a new Reaper. He had been there before any of the others, and once his hundred years was up, he had stayed on to train new Reapers in their art. A short, tanned man with perfectly slicked-back brunette hair, he made up for his stature with a merry, Mediterranean-accented voice and enthusiastic hand gestures. Ryder liked him instantly for his genuine charm.

Ryder pointed towards the swirling cycle of purple energy, perfectly poised above a large, circular stone platform, decorated with tiny skulls and bursts of fire. "This thing?"

Greek twisted back, fixing him with a stern glare, one hand on his hip in an authoritative manner. "Yes, that *thing*. It's called a Catcher, remember?" He sighed again. "Do try to remember the names, I'm not repeating myself all day." Twisting around again, he busied himself by a far table. The heavy mahogany affair was laden under a pile of metal objects and weapons, several scythes at the far end.

Striding across to run his hand over the cool metal of the curved heads, Ryder's eyes gleamed at the selection, asking excitedly, "So do I get one of these? They look awesome."

He was shocked by a sharp slap across his hand, stinging as Greek tutted in warning. "I did not say you could touch things. Don't touch the things. Okay? And no, you don't get one." Greek gave a wry smile, his bronzed face lighting with the motion. "We stopped using these...oh, sometime after the Black Death. People just got too freaked out by them. Besides, they're old school."

"Yeah," Ryder added, casting his gaze around the gothic decoration of the room as he shoved his hands into his jean pockets, a repeat of the grand marble from the Hall of Rest, with heavy timber across the sky-like ceiling. "I'd noticed you guys like old school."

Greek gave a snort, his smart black shirt rustling as he snatched up a few items from the table before following Ryder's stare. "Don't blame me. I didn't decorate this place. *I* wanted Italian silks and pearl surfaces, but they said it was too much trouble."

Ryder grinned at Greek's humour, chuckling as the shorter man steered him over to the platform with a pile of objects in one arm. Pulling Ryder's hands from his pockets, he laid something that resembled a silver gun in his palm, his features growing serious. "Now, no joking around about this one. It's a weapon, but I don't ever want to hear of you using it if you don't have to."

"What is it? A gun? Seems rather pointless when you're already dead," Ryder quipped, arching a jet-black eyebrow as he studied the weapon, turning it over in his hands.

"It's not a gun," Greek explained patiently, tapping it with one finger. "It's a...well, it's a kind of stun gun. You might need it if anyone else tries to take the soul you're collecting."

The mysterious 'someone else' again. Curiosity piqued once again, Ryder jutted his chin towards his companion, tightening his grasp on the stun gun. "Ankou and Morrigan mentioned something about that. When is someone going to tell me what the hell it is I might have to go up against?"

Greek paused in his task, lowering his eyes and carefully placing the objects in his arms onto the table once more. Flicking his gaze over towards the Hall of Rest, he came in closer, his tone dropping as he murmured, "They're called 'Warders'. There's another realm, called Helheim. Queen Empusa reigns over it, and she requires souls to become Warders for her, or to do who knows what in Helheim itself." With a shiver, he continued, "It's not a good place. You'll know them if you see them though. Humans can't tell them apart from themselves, but you'll see their true form." He raised his eyes again, jabbing a finger towards Ryder's face. "Demonic creatures, you can't miss them. If you see them, point that at them, pull the trigger, and run."

Swallowing anxiously, Ryder gave a curt nod, bringing the gun to his back and tucking it in his waistband. The cold steel sent a thrill through his skin, adding to the trepidation roiling in the pit of his stomach. It wasn't as though he hadn't held or used a gun before, but he had never come up against a demonic being in his short lifetime. Jerking his head towards the other objects, he asked quietly, "What about these things? Do I need these too?"

Brightening as they broke away from the ominous conversation, Greek gave a breezy smile, pulling up a small black mobile phone and waving it in front of him. "You'll need this. It's how you get to Earth and back to here. When there's an incoming call, just answer it. It'll take you where you're needed most. Sometimes you might have to search a while, but it'll always take you nearby." He demonstrated by punching a few numbers, directing Ryder's attention to the gleaming flatscreen. "And...press this red one when you want to return here. Easy." Slipping it into Ryder's pocket, he clapped his hands together in delight, urging with his eyebrows for his trainee to stand on the platform behind.

"A mobile phone?" Ryder repeated sceptically, peering into his pocket at the device. "Seems at odds with all this."

"Yes, yes, we've had this talk already. Just be grateful you're not being given a staff to carry around, those were *heavy*." Greek waved him backwards, tapping his foot impatiently. "Let's get a move on, you're not my only person to see today, lovely as you are. Let's get going, your work awaits."

"Hang on!" Ryder protested, his booted foot catching the edge of the circular disc, stumbling as he righted himself. The purple mist eddied around him, whispering as it gathered like flies on honey. "You mean, that's it? I'm to go right now?"

Greek surveyed him with his wide grin, letting out a merry peal of laughter. "Of course! What did you think, that you would stand around all day and look at shiny objects? This isn't a museum, even if it looks the part—against my better judgement, I must say."

"But I'm not ready, I don't know what to say. What do I—"

His protests were cut off by Greek heaving a dramatic sigh and leaning across, hitting the green button of the mobile device as a shrill tune rung out from it. "You'll be fine! Be yourself."

The voice of the cheerful trainer faded into darkness as Ryder was sucked downwards in a spiral of purple magic. The air was sucked from his lungs as he sailed downwards, his arms and hair lifting against his will as the updraft caught him, twisting him in its wind. Feeling like Alice descending into the rabbit hole, Ryder tried to hold onto his guts as the contents within them roiled, the strong wind whistling past his ears in a banshee's cry.

Hitting the hard ground below, Ryder choked out a wheezing breath, clutching at his chest. Blinking hard, he glanced up towards the sky, expecting to see the strange tunnel he had tunnelled through, but his gaze was met with only the soothing winks of the stars above in a dark night sky. Ryder let out a calming breath, breathing in and out until his pulse slowed down again and let his heart ease away from his ribs. Picking himself up from the gritty pavement, he took a look around, taking in his surroundings.

He was stood at the corner of a suburban street, lined either side with modern red-brick houses, each with their uniformly coordinating doors and windows. BMWs were parked snugly next to Volvos, all gleaming outside the garages they never rested in. It was exactly the kind of neighbourhood Ryder always used to either avoid, or trash if he got the chance. Rubbing a hand across his face tiredly, he cracked his neck, reaching up to pull the collar of his jacket around his neck.

Time to get to work, I guess.

CHAPTER FOUR

Setting off at a strong pace, Ryder passed his cool eyes from house to house, wandering along aimlessly between the identical buildings. Scratching his head, he paused for a moment and shook his head, muttering to himself. "How the fuck am I supposed to know which house it is?"

Letting out a loud curse, he twisted around on the spot, gazing towards each door as if it would light up and let off a siren for him. Scanning a bright red door across the street, he narrowed his eyes, something about it standing out amongst the others. The fine hairs rose on the back of his neck, and his lips parted as he realised it was *the* house. *I can't explain it...I guess it's a gut feeling, after all.* Allowing the confidence of his decision to fill him, he made his way over, the streetlights from above casting an orange glow on his figure.

Reaching the cheerful front door, he put a hand out to grasp the knob, preparing to push hard against the lock that would surely be in place on the other side. But as he reached for the handle, his hand slipped straight through the wood to the inside of the house. Letting out a sharp yell, he tumbled through to a plush beige carpet, holding his arms out to prevent his face meeting the floor on closer terms. Glancing back at his legs, still cut off by the door and hanging outside, he grumbled, "Guess I don't need to use doors, then."

Scooping himself off the floor, Ryder dusted himself off and took in his surroundings. It was a neat, tidy house, but the decorating was a few decades out of date, faded yellow wallpaper covered in bright blue stripes and pine furniture. It was obvious an old lady resided here, judging by the varied collection of porcelain ornaments that were dotted artfully over tables and windowsills. Ryder smiled wistfully as he trailed his fingers over the hand-painted surface of a milkmaid's rosy face. A sound came from upstairs, like a floorboard creaking, and he glanced up towards it with watchful eyes. The tattoo sprang into life on his skin, burning his flesh with a warning reminder of why he was here.

Hissing as he clamped his spare hand around the sleeve, Ryder took a deep breath and placed his foot on the first stair upwards. It didn't make a sound under his weight, and he continued up the narrow staircase, looking from left to right as he reached the unlit landing at the top. Pictures were strewn across the walls, a myriad of happy, smiling faces. Some of the pictures were black and white, taken from an era where wearing an evening gown was natural for a photo, right up to modern digital outputs with a beaming, wrinkled old lady. The resemblance was too much for it not to be the same woman, but she was joined along her own personal timeline by more faces, children, grandchildren, nieces, nephews…a long family line of love and warm memories.

A sob came from his left, followed by a soothing murmur of sympathy. Trepidation fluttering his heart into life, Ryder crept along the landing until he came across what he could only assume was the old lady's bedroom. The sight was heart-breaking. The room itself was soft pink, and the main theme throughout was roses; in vases, on wallpaper, on the bedspread. A frail old woman lay in the centre of the bed, the merest of breaths barely moving her chest, her curling white hair resting against a soft pillow. She was surrounded by loved ones, so many of them that they struggled to squeeze into the small room.

Ryder spotted the source of the sob, a young woman in a blue cardigan, crying into the chest of a tall man by her side, who stroked her hair and whispered soothing words into her ear. An older lady, the spitting image of the woman lying in the bed—presumably a daughter—was perched on the edge of the mattress. Tears streamed down her cheeks as she clutched her mother's hand tightly, but a cheerful smile was on her lips. All the relatives looked the same, their attention directed towards the figure, the matriarch of their universe, salty water leaving tracks on their drawn faces.

A lump formed in Ryder's throat at the sight, and he swallowed it back bitterly, his mouth tightening into a scowl. The resentment at his own family rose up once more, as he considered the possibility they hadn't even bothered to find him if they knew he was dead. Shaking his head free of the thoughts, he roved his gaze around the room, unsure what to do next. Then someone caught his eye. It was the old lady from the bed, a confused frown furrowing her already deep wrinkles, pulling a long white nightdress tightly around her frail form.

That must be her. Uncertainty prickling under his skin, Ryder squeezed through the mass of people, finding that unlike the door, he didn't glide through them like a ghost. Making his way to the woman's side, he cleared his throat, gazing down at her with a stern frown. She turned wide hazel eyes to him, letting out a whimper as a gnarled hand flew to her mouth. "Hey. Are you the old lady down there?" Ryder jerked his head over to the bed, pointing sharply.

"I...I'm not sure," she whispered in a shaking voice. "I think so. Who are you? Please tell me what's happening." Her trembling hand clutched fearfully at her nightgown, and her lip wobbled as tears formed at the corners of her eyes. "I can't talk to any of them. They won't listen."

Ryder blew out a harsh breath. This was harder than he thought it would be. Giving a curt nod, he gazed down at his scuffed leather boots and replied, "Yes. You're dead. My name's Ryder, and I have to take you away now." Grasping her arm as tightly as he dared, lest her thin bones broke under his hold, he reached into his pocket for the mobile device.

"No! Wait!" The old lady cried, dragging her arm from his grasp. Shaking her head vigorously, she explained, "I can't go yet. I have to say goodbye. Please."

Turning his face away for a moment so that she couldn't see him blinking rapidly to stop the flood of tears from her statement, Ryder relented. "Alright. But make it quick."

"Thank you, young man," the woman croaked gratefully, laying a tiny, wrinkled hand on his arm. "And my name is Abigail, if you need to know." Ignoring his shrug to her introduction, she made her way across to her daughter perched on the bed, laying a hand against her cheek. Her thumb passed over the tear streaks as though she could wipe them away, but they remained in their glistening tracks. Pressing a kiss to the woman's forehead, she murmured, "Rebecca, my darling daughter. I'm so proud of you, and of the wonderful man you chose, my son-in-law. And your children! I've been so lucky to have such amazing grandchildren. So lucky."

Ryder gave a snort before he could stop himself, the shield of anger slamming back into place over his emotions. Abigail spun her head around to fix him with a cold glare, her fear melting away into stern authority.

"Young man! How dare you."

"What?" Ryder demanded, his tone harsher than he had meant it to sound. Shrugging his shoulders causally as he buried his hands in his pockets, he continued, "It's a load of crap, anyway. You think they're going to remember you in a couple of years' time? Three? Five? I hate to burst your bubble, lady, but life goes on. And it goes on without us."

For a second, Abigail looked as though she was about to reproach him, but she clamped her mouth shut. Taking a second to smile around at the sea of faces watching her aged body, she rose carefully, striding across to Ryder and placing a soft hand on his arm. Startled by the movement, he jumped at her touch, staring down at the gnarled hand with wide eyes. Sighing sadly, Abigail uttered, "Young man...Ryder...I'm sorry for whoever hurt you. No one should feel like that about their life. I know I was lucky, very lucky, to have had such a wonderful life and family over the years. I did everything I wanted to do, and have loving children and grandchildren." The tears finally slipped from her gentle eyes, and she gave a sniff, squeezing his arm. "I hope they *do* forget about this. At least my death. I only want them to remember the good times with me, when I was alive enough to do things with them. Not this, as a frail old lady."

Ryder's jaw tensed as he gazed down at her, regret washing over him for how he had spoken to her. "I'm sorry, I didn't mean it like that."

"I know, young man, I know." Abigail patted his arm and grinned up at him, her face lighting up, a distant reminder of the merry young woman she had once been. "It is not whether we are remembered, it is whether we know we did all we could with our lives. No one is ever forgotten, however much you think you might be. I certainly won't forget you." Her hand came up to pat his cheek, and she let out a laden sigh. "Is it time then?"

Lowering his head and placing an arm awkwardly around her shoulders, Ryder gave a wry smile and whispered, "I'm afraid so. You're going somewhere wonderful though." He hugged the old lady into his body, wishing someone had spoken to him as she had done when he was alive. *But at least now I have a chance to do just that. No one will remember me, but I'll know I set it right.* Abigail gave a last loving glance to her family, heaving out a contended sigh. Placing his hand into his jacket pocket, Ryder drew out the mobile device and hit the red button, bracing himself as he waited for the inevitable rush of wind and energy.

To his surprise, instead of the wind tunnel of crackling energy, a soft white light descended around them both. It glowed brighter until it was almost blinding to look at, humming softly with sweet, musical voices, lifting Abigail and Ryder from the floor towards the ceiling. They passed through it as though it was made of air, sailing higher and higher into the other realm that held the Hall of Rest. Ryder placed an arm over his eyes, blocking out the brilliance as it burst into a resounding explosion of light, before dissipating and revealing the black marble floor of the hall.

"Damn," he muttered to himself. "They'll do that now, but I had to go down the fucking tunnel of wonders."

"Young man!" Abigail admonished with a shocked furrow of her brow. Wagging her finger at him, she added, "Has anyone ever told you that you swear too much?" Her features softening, she paused, and reached up to pat his cheek again. "Don't worry, Ryder. It'll be alright in the end. You'll see. Things always work themselves out."

Ankou and Morrigan swept across in a flurry of feathers and heavy cloak, their hands outstretched to Abigail. Nodding over to Ryder, Morrigan cast him a soft smile, remarking, "You did well, Ryder. We'll take Abigail from here. Thank you." Waving goodbye, Abigail allowed herself to be led away by the two guardians, over towards the pool that would show her next life.

As Ryder stared after their retreating figures, he clutched at his chest as it tightened for a second in worry. *I hope her next life is as beautiful as her last one.* The sudden thought shocked him, and he shook his head, willing himself not to dwell on it. He gave a grunt to no one in particular, twisting on his heel and storming off towards the training area. For the first time in his life — afterlife or not — he wondered if he should have been so ready to blame everyone but himself for his circumstances.

CHAPTER FIVE

Greek swept through the chambers with a rustle of pink silk, his choice of shirt for the day. Spying Ryder sat by himself at a table with his feet up on the surface, he rushed across, his steps echoing off the walls. Ryder sat twirling an apple in his fingers on the table's surface, gazing at it vacantly as it swivelled under his touch. The chambers were nice enough, a simple affair for all new Reapers-In-Training, lighter and less opulent than the rest of the Hall of Rest. Bunks were spread across one wall, each one with neatly folded sheets, with tall lockers residing between each set of beds. A large oak table sat in the centre, looking more like a prop from a medieval play than a dining area for reapers.

It was etched with the graffiti of reapers no longer living there, and Ryder absentmindedly traced one of them with his spare hand, not noticing as Greek halted next to his arm. As the older man cleared his throat, Ryder gave a start, the apple rolling out of his fingers as he hurriedly brought his boots down off the table. Leaning down to catch it, Ryder sat back up with a red face, apologising, "Sorry, Greek, I didn't see you there."

Waving a hand in a dismissive manner, Greek shook his head as he rolled his eyes to the low white ceiling. "Oh, young man, no one ever notices me when I need to speak to them. And I do need to speak to you. You're officially being sent back down to Earth."

Ryder leaned back in the chair, creaking under his weight as he linked his hands together, his blue-black quiff bobbing at his sudden movement. Quirking an eyebrow in his usual casual style, he echoed, "Down to Earth? I don't understand."

Perching himself down onto the edge of the worn surface, Greek folded his arms over his chest and gave a solemn nod. "Yes, down to the big place. There's a small group of reapers who live down there permanently, about the same age as you. Well, they died at about your age, anyway. We thought you might be more comfortable there—as well as less bored—if you were around others in your situation." Gesturing around the empty chambers, he explained, "It's been a slow year for reapers. Not everyone wants to take on the duties, you know." Lifting himself up again, he tossed a jangling set of keys in front of Ryder with a grin. "These are for you. A little present."

Frowning, Ryder leaned forwards and scooped up the keys, holding them up to gleam in the electric light from above, inspecting them closely. As he twisted them over, he caught sight of a familiar badge, one that quickened his heartbeat. *Ducati.* He took in a sharp breath, glancing up at Greek with shining eyes. "Is this what I think it is?"

Letting out a chuckle, Greek slapped a hand against Ryder's back, his dark hair flopping artfully across one eye. "It is. As your bike got damaged, we thought you might like a new one. You know, to look more stylish when you're rolling around picking those souls up. It won't do to take the bus."

"Wow. Er…thanks." Ryder bit his lip, rolling the keys over in his palm as though he couldn't believe they were there, a grin breaking out across his lips. "I mean, really, thanks. No one ever gave me anything before. It's really mine?"

Greek raised his eyebrows in mock surprise, holding his hands up. "Well it's not mine. I don't travel by anything less than limousine or flying horse, thank you very much." Dropping the dramatic act for a moment, he squeezed Ryder's shoulder affectionately. "Enjoy it. And don't smash this one up."

"No fear," Ryder retorted vehemently, a flashback of the terrible smash coming back to haunt him. Shaking himself free of the memory, he scraped his chair back loudly, pocketing the keys with a practised movement. Nodding over to the training room, with the platform of energy, he queried, "Shall I get going then?"

"Of course. But don't forget your duties. You've got a night off, to get yourself settled in. Then it's back to work tomorrow."

At Greek's words, Ryder paused, running a hand over his quiff. Drumming his fingers against the hip of his rough jeans, he asked quietly, "Greek?"

The short Mediterranean man spun around on his way through, searching Ryder's earnest face with inquisitive, dark eyes as he waited for what the younger man wanted. "Yes?"

"You know that old woman...Abigail?"

Greek eyes narrowed, and he crossed his arms again, tilting his chin back in an authoritative manner. "What about her?"

Ryder nervously tapped his foot, giving a Gallic shrug as he mumbled, "Well...I just wanted to know if she was okay. In her new life, I mean."

His companion's face melted into emotion, and Greek came across, placing both hands on Ryder's cheeks. Giving them a sharp, friendly tap of approval, he cocked his head and smiled wistfully. "I'm sorry, Ryder. I just don't know, I'm afraid. But I think her next life was a good one. She will be loved."

"Good." Ryder gave a firm nod, as though

cementing this fact in his head. "I just wanted to know. She...she seemed like a nice lady. I just want to know she didn't—that is, I didn't bring her to—anything terrible."

"You're going soft on me," Greek remarked wryly, giving a wink. "Don't lose your edge, Ryder, you might like it."

Snorting derisively at Greek's comment, Ryder breezed past him wordlessly, making his way through the corridor to the training area beyond the chambers. But he felt his heart lifting at the thought that sweet old Abigail was going onto a good life again. *Maybe there's hope for me yet.*

Thrown out onto the hard granite below, Ryder swore loudly and gingerly picked himself up, rubbing his sore behind. "I am never going to get used to that," he muttered. The Tunnel of Wonders, as he had sarcastically termed it, wasn't getting any more comfortable to travel along.

Ryder rubbed at his dry, tired eyes, blinking as he stared ahead at the beautiful steel beast that was now his, and his alone. It was another Ducati, like his smashed one had been, but it gleamed wickedly with polished chrome and dark blue hues. A grinning skull, set against a blast of flame, decorated the body. Chrome instruments dotted the dashboard with old school pointers and large numbers. A smirk curled his lips as he stared at it, roving his cool eyes across it appreciatively. "Hell, yes. You little beauty."

Striding across purposely, he yanked the keys from his pocket, catching them on the jacket lining in his haste Hooking his leg over the seat, he clunked the keys into place and turned the ignition. The engine roared into life like a caged beast, growling as he placed his hands firmly on the handlebars, knocking the kickstand as he had done so many times before. Ryder knew where to go, thanks to actually being given directions this time, and he thrust the motorbike forwards with a delighted laugh.

Taking care to go slower than the fateful night he died, Ryder breathed in the air rushing past his face, revving the bike as he curved around corners and buildings with ease. Greek had let him know that he could be seen at all times by the human population when not on a collection, but doors and entrances would open for him like Ali Baba's cave if he wished to go through. It was a strange sensation, to be in charge of such magical power, and Ryder had to remind himself that the next hundred years might be even harder than his first collection.

Heading for the east side of town, he took in his surroundings. They were familiar, places he had often hung out when he was alive. The 'bad' side of town. *Well, cheaper, anyway.* Council houses and high-rise flats rubbed shoulders with grimy strip clubs and battered charity shops, broken only by the occasional takeaway shop, lit up to draw in the late-night revellers falling out of the pubs.

Checking the address in his head, he slowed the bike as he drew up in front of a discarded building. It was set away from the main road down a side-street, once surrounded by bustling shops, now all boarded-up and left to rot. He bumped the bike up the kerb, pulling it into the large carpark out the front of the building as he looked up with uncertainty. Once a popular pool club, the battered 1960's building was boarded up with graffitied sheets of substitute wood, its sign faded and scratched with age. The glass window set in the main door had a large crack down the centre, and an attempt to fix it had been made with packing tape, but the effect was pitiful. As the engine died with a final growl, Ryder slid off the seat, swinging the keys around his index finger as he made his way across. He listened intently for any sounds of life, but the place seemed as deserted as it looked. *Is this the right place? Looks like a right shithole. Still, I've woken up in worse places.*

Straightening his spine, he raised his hand, and rapped tersely on the door. Silence greeted him. Ryder ground his teeth together in impatience, taking a step back and screwing his face against the sun as he raised icy eyes to view the upper floor of the building. Letting out an exasperated sigh, he returned to the door and knocked again, hammering loud enough to rattle the broken glass in its frame. Still silence.

Losing all patience, he pressed his flat palm against the wood, and slid through the door to the other side. As his eyes adjusted to the darkness of the musty room within, he heard an audible click to his right, the cocking of a handgun. Automatically throwing his hands up in surrender, Ryder slowly turned his head to gaze down the barrel of a stun gun identical to his own. It was held by a towering young man with closely-shaven dark hair, his vivid green eyes glaring into Ryder's skull.

As the two stared at one another, the six-foot-something giant gave a relieved sigh, pulling the stun gun away, his shoulders relaxing. "It's alright, everyone. It's just the new guy." There were sounds of stun guns being clicked off, and shuffling feet from the main area beyond the dingy hallway they stood in.

Lowering his arms, pulse rushing through his veins with the adrenaline from being held at gunpoint, Ryder raised an eyebrow. "Nice. You greet all newcomers this way?"

Green Eyes jutted his chin up, resting the stun gun over one shoulder, still gripping it tightly as he swaggered past Ryder into the room. "Sorry, mate," he apologised casually. "We heard the bike, didn't know who it was. Thought you might be a Warder. Go on through."

Following the tall man's careless gesture, Ryder made his way into the main area, picking over cardboard boxes and rubbish strewn on the floor. The meagre light came from a few bare bulbs hanging from the ceiling, one of them swaying in a ghostly breeze that drifted through the space nonchalantly. Five other figures stood in defensive poses around the room, each one with a searching look on their faces. Two large pool tables stood at one end, one of them with a vicious tear down its centre, plastered down with the same packing tape that fluttered across the front door. Moth-eaten sofas were carelessly arranged around a small heater, a large fridge humming away behind one of them, looking as though it had been the featured product of an era when *rock-n-roll* was king. A single, battered television stood in the corner, lines jumping across the screen erratically as the smiling face of a weather girl appeared behind the static snow.

Waving a hand in a deferential greeting, Ryder passed his gaze between each person in turn. "Great to meet you all. Friendly bunch, aren't you?"

A woman in a long belted shirt slunk out from the corner, sliding her stun gun into the side of the belt as she studied him with a sneer. "It's necessary if we want to survive. So you're the new guy, huh? You don't look like much to me. A stiff breeze might knock you over. Still...reapers are reapers." Clasping her hand over her chest, she continued in a stern tone, "I'm Alisha. Not 'Ali', not 'Sha', *Alisha*. I don't need a friggin' nickname."

"Ryder," he replied tartly, jabbing a thumb

towards himself. "Just...er, Ryder."

Aisha snorted, tossing her short red bob out of her eyes. "Ryder? Is that some sort of hint towards the bike?"

Narrowing his eyes at the feisty woman, he snarled, "No. It was my grandfather's name."

"Alright, cool it down in here," Green Eyes warned, coming through and squeezing his massive frame past Ryder, pointing towards Alisha. She stared at him with venom, giving an exasperated sigh before turning and flopping onto a sofa. Twisting back, Green Eyes pointed to himself and added, "I'm Gabe. Don't mind Alisha, she's prickly to everyone. We don't think it's catching though. Beer?" Without waiting for an answer, he strode across to the humming fridge, yanking it open and pulling out two bottles, throwing one across to Ryder.

"Cheers," Ryder called back, catching the dripping bottle with ease and cracking the top against the wall, popping the cap off. Knocking back a slug of the icy nectar within, he nodded towards the other figures. "And you guys?"

Two nearly identical men stepped forwards, both with peroxide-blonde hair and soft coffee eyes. They were dressed in ripped t-shirts and jeans, both with spiked hair that made them look like a young Billy Idol tribute act. One of them tilted his chin at Ryder with a broad grin, introducing himself, "I'm Drew, and this is my twin, Devin. Good to meet you, Ryder."

Ryder saluted them back with his beer bottle, smiling back at the genuine greeting. "Twins? How did that work?"

Devin's face fell, and he wrapped an arm around his brother's shoulder with a sigh. "Let's just say drugs work, and leave it at that. Not proud of it."

Fuck. I forgot about the whole 'sudden death' thing. Watch what you say, Ryder thought to himself with an apologetic wince. He didn't have long to think about it as the final two figures came into view from the far end of the room, one of them plumping down onto an over-stuffed seat, both women. The woman on the sofa was tall and broad, but still shorter than both Gabe and Ryder, her long black hair falling across her shoulders as she stared coldly back towards him. The other woman was petite and slim, her dark hair curling into tight afro-ringlets against her caramel skin.

"I'm Mika, and this is McKenna," the woman on the sofa commented, nodding her head towards the petite woman.

"Nice to meet you, Ryder," McKenna added, offering a warm smile. "Guess this makes us seven, then. More the merrier, as far as I'm concerned. We're short of cute guys around here." She giggled mischievously and gave a playful wink, chuckling to herself at the raised eyebrow from Gabe. "Welcome to the Grim Alliance."

"The 'Grim Alliance'? Really?"

Drew gave a chuckle at Ryder's question. "It was that or 'Deaths R' Us'. That had less of a catchy ring to it."

As the group descended to the sofas, Gabe waved Ryder across, splashing his beer onto his arm with the movement. "Come sit down, mate. Tell us about yourself."

"Er, okay." Ryder confidently walked over to the centre of the group watching him intently, easing himself down onto the edge of a worn cushion as he knocked back another swig of his refreshing drink. Smacking his lips together in satisfaction, he leaned against the back of the sofa, and surveyed the intense faces staring back at him. "Okay. My real name is Gilbert, but nobody calls me that.

It's Ryder, my middle name." He cast Alisha a scowl, but she simply crossed her arms and grinned back patronisingly. "I only died recently, in a motorbike crash. I was...I was being chased by the cops. I woke up in the Hall of Rest, and that's how I became a reaper."

"Woah there, Speedy Gonzales," Alisha interrupted, raising her eyebrows and wiggling her head from side to side as she held her hands up. "You've left out a lot of stuff there. What about your family? Why were you being chased by the police?"

"Alisha, why don't you shut up?" Devin warned, glaring across at her with a darkening expression.

"What? I'm just asking the guy a few questions."

Ryder held his hand up to indicate silence, keeping the peace. Stretching his legs out and crossing them, he shook his head. "No, it's fine. I've nothing to hide. My parents are arseholes. My father's been drunk since the day I was born, and it gives him one hell of a temper. He used to take it out on my mother and me, beating us if he lost on the horses, any reason really." His fists tightened in response to his words, and his blue eyes hardened into ice. "When I was sixteen, and finally bigger, I took a swing at him. Landed him on the floor, then I left. Haven't seen him since."

Mika angled her head back at him, her expression softening at his story. "What about your mum?"

"She wasn't any better." Ryder rolled his thumb over the neck of the bottle, studying it as though it might hold a better answer than any he could give. "She always got drunk when he did, said she did it so she couldn't feel his fist as much. Whenever she could, she would run out on us, leaving me behind. Fuck knows where she went, I think she just shacked up with anything that would take her in for the night. When I left, I hadn't seen her for about two years. I don't know if she came back or not. I got into trouble with the law from when I was a kid, fell in with a gang...I wasn't exactly given a fair chance in life though." He tossed his shoulders, emptying his drink and twisting the empty bottle in his hand. As he raised his eyes, he was fixed with the sadness in the gazes of his listeners, and he gave a wry smile. "Look, it's nothing to weep about, okay? Shit happens."

"Yeah, but...why didn't you change it when you left? Left home, I mean?" McKenna spoke up, perching herself on the arm of the sofa, swallowing anxiously at Ryder's glare of contention. "I'm just wondering."

"I said," he bit out through gritted teeth, "I didn't exactly get a fair chance." Placing the bottle down by his feet, he leapt up from the cushion, dust flying off in a great cloud. Nearly stumbling as he kicked his way over the layers of rubbish, he caught himself in time and made a beeline for the exit. "Fuck this. I didn't come here for the Spanish Inquisition."

Gabe raced in front of him, catching his arm just as he reached the entry to the hallway, leaning in. "Ryder, don't go. No one's trying to get you riled. Well, maybe Alisha, but like I said, she's kind of a bitch. In the most loving way possible. We're just curious." He gave a one-sided grin, shrugging easily. "You know how nosy people are. And besides...you're our brother now." Gabe slapped his hand down onto Ryder's shoulders heavily, making the shorter man balk under the sudden weight.

Ryder blinked for a few seconds, glancing back over his shoulder. Even Alisha managed to look suitably ashamed, and McKenna's eyes were cast down to the floor. He glanced over each of them in silence, forcing his anger to simmer down again. Running his tongue over his lips, Ryder bent his head, twisting back with a laden sigh. "Alright. I'm just not ready to talk about all that yet. Okay? Sorry if I seem guarded, but...I am."

"I really didn't mean to piss you off or anything," McKenna garbled in a rush, wringing her hands. It was obvious to see she was the tender heart of the group, sensitive to how her words might be taken. Ryder's chest tightened at the thought he had been upset over something so—now, anyway—insignificant.

"It's wasn't you," he smiled wryly. "It's me. I'm still touchy about it." *Why am I so touchy about it? It was just a question.*

"We've all got into shit of some kind here," Alisha remarked, grinning widely for the first time since he had entered. The smile lit up her heart-shaped face, and took away some of the resentful anger that lingered on her brow, leaving the hopeful face of a twenty-something. Jabbing a thumb into her chest, she continued, "I did drugs. Hard stuff, too. Sold it, took it, ran out, prostituted myself, everything. Then one New Year's Eve when I was alone, I took too much of it, and I ended up in the Hall of Rest." She shook her head, casting her eyes down to her worn trainers. "The thing is, it was only once I'd died that I realised all the bad stuff I'd caused, all the people I might have injured or killed with the drugs. Becoming a reaper was the best thing I've ever done in my life." Alisha raised her fierce gaze again, locking storm-grey eyes with Ryder, the vehemence of her words clear in her expression.

"Same with us," Drew perked up, jerking his head towards his brother, now crouched on the sofa with his knees drawn to his chin. "We did what we liked, so long as we did it together. We used to punch a different group of guys up every night. Drinking, taking drugs...it was part of the lifestyle for our band. It was the Eighties, everyone we knew did it. Then one night..." he trailed off, swallowing hard as his jaw ticked.

Seeing his twin's reluctance to finish the story, Devin laid a hand on his arm, rubbing it affectionately. It obvious that the two of them were closer to each other than anyone else in the group. Looking across to Ryder, who was listening intently with a solemn face, he picked up the tale again in a low tone. "We did something terrible one night. But you've got to understand, we didn't *know* what we were doing. There were a couple of girls with us, you know, *in bed*. Both Drew and I had the same bad batch of heroin, and we both hallucinated that we'd grown wings. We went out onto the balcony, opened our arms...and that's how we ended up here."

Ryder nearly gave a shrug, but stopped himself in time, instead choosing his words with more care than usual. "That's not so terrible—that didn't come out right. I mean, it's terrible, but you didn't harm anyone but yourselves."

Devin shook his head mournfully, his features darkening. "You don't understand. We...made the girls do it with us. In our hallucination, they were laughing and giggling about it. It wasn't until we all landed in the Hall of Rest that we realised what had happened. They went on to their next lives, but Drew and I knew we had to make up for what we'd done."

"We're all the same," Gabe commented, placing his bottle down on a table and leaning himself on the edge, folding his arms over his chest. "So don't worry about what we'll think of you. None of us would be here if we hadn't done something to warrant it."

Ryder arched an eyebrow in his usual fashion, twisting to stare across at McKenna, wet cardboard tearing under his feet. "Even you? You don't seem the type—I mean that nicely."

She chewed on a strand of her hair for a moment silently, worrying at it as she gave a single nod. "Even me. A guy tried to rape me, so I defended myself. The only thing I could get hold of in that dark alleyway was a shard of glass, and I stabbed him with it. I stabbed him over and over, just to get his filthy weight off me. I was scared, I hardly knew what I was doing. It screwed me up. When it went to court, they said I'd done it on purpose, not in self-defence. That I had led the guy on, and he had thought it was consensual. And...because I was black, it ended there."

"What?" Ryder scowled at the injustice. "That's fucking messed up."

McKenna looked away, her fingers coming down to toy with the buttons on her orange cardigan. "It was the Sixties, no one really cared what a black woman had to say, Ryder. Times are—and have—changed considerably, and I'm glad. But when I was raped, some people still believed that dressing a certain way 'asked for it'. That being black somehow made me less worthy of justice." The fingers twitched ever faster. "And when I was left alone one night in my cell, when all the guards were off watching the New Year's fireworks out in the yard.. well, I had a razor blade. You can work out the rest."

"McKenna, I'm so sorry," Ryder murmured, his heart going out to the nervous young woman —although by her story, really she was at least sixty —breaking for what had happened to her. "What I went through is nothing compared to you." He swivelled his head around the group, gesturing causally with open arms. "Really, not compared to any of you. I shouldn't complain."

Gabe cleared his throat loudly, clearing away

some of the oppressive, mournful fog that had settled over the gang. Pointing up above his head to the peeling paint on the ceiling, he announced, "The bedroom is upstairs. You can go up and choose a bed, if you want. It's not much, but it's all ours. It's the one with all the beds and stuff in, not the others."

"Thanks. I'll do that now," Ryder replied quietly, grateful for any reason to excuse himself. He hadn't meant to cause such a downswing in the group's mood, but it guessed it was par for the course, at least for a while. It wasn't as if anyone there hadn't been in the same position as him at some point.

He made his way back out into the dim hallway, spotting the stairs at the far end, darker and covered in a ratty green carpet that didn't quite reach the width of each step. Hearing a buzz of conversation starting up again in the main area, Ryder continued upstairs and took the steps two at a time, racing towards the landing. It was much the same as the hallway below, badly lit and covered in debris from previous residents, with seven doors leading off from it. A quick glance into two of the doors confirmed they were bathrooms, four others were single dilapidated bedrooms, with the last one leading to the shared bedroom.

As Ryder stepped inside, he had to blink at the sudden bursts of light through the windows, all of them larger than the ones downstairs and flooding the room with evening sunshine. Metal-framed beds were lined up either side of the room, rather like a dormitory, scruffy but clean sheets laid haphazard on each one. Three of the beds were separated from the rest by a makeshift room divider, created from loose interior doors and wooden signs, scavenged from outside. He assumed those were the beds for the women, and made his way towards the other side.

The three men's beds were a complete mess, the personality of its inhabitant plastered firmly into the space around each one. The first two clearly belonged to Devin and Drew, the beds drawn together just a little closer than the others, the only difference what was strewn between them on the floor. One side was littered with 'lad's mags', brazen pictures of semi-naked woman covering the pages, while the other bed was carpeted by piles of books, some leather-bound and some worn paperbacks, all lovingly stacked together.

Gabe's bed came after them, the only one where some attempt to keep the sheets tidy had been made. There was no mess on the floor either, only a few books and knick-knacks on the windowsill behind the headboard. Ryder peered in at the myriad of objects, many of them seeming out of place for a gruff, shaven-headed giant of a man. There were several photos in a pile, but Ryder left those. It felt too much like intruding to gaze at someone else's memories. His hands lighted on a snowglobe, a small glass ball with an angelic scene inside of winter. Two tiny figures laughed and skated with one another on a gleaming ice-rink, the background made up of tall buildings and the announcement, 'Welcome to Denmark'. He tipped it upside down and twirled it back around, watching as the glittering pieces of fake snow slowly fell back onto the floor of the miniature panorama, leaving an innocent sense of wonderment. As he swayed it back and forth to recreate the snow, a sharp rap at the doorway nearly made him drop the globe, slipping from his hands before he caught it in time.

Breathing hard to regain his calm, pulse zipping under his skin like a live wire, Ryder placed the globe hurriedly back on the windowsill like a guilty child and spun around. He was met with the lopsided grin and raised eyebrows of Alisha, arms folded across her chest as she held back laughter at his shock. "Bit nosy, aren't you?" she quipped, releasing her arms as she came into the room, striding over to Gabe's bedside. "You shouldn't go poking around other people's things."

"I wasn't poking around," Ryder insisted, shoving his hands deep into his pockets and taking a step back. "I just spotted it, that's all. I loved those things as a kid."

Alisha gave a soft smile as she cast her eyes over the small object, letting out a chuckle. "Yeah, I did too." Fixing Ryder with her intense gaze, her expression grew solemn. "But don't let Gabe catch you touching it. His stuff is strictly out of bounds. The guy might tell you about it one day. He's got good reason for it."

Giving a firm nod, Ryder replied, "No problem. I'll remember."

"Look, I'm sorry for being a bitch. It's just my armour, okay?"

Ryder flashed Alisha a winning grin, his cool eyes glittering with mischief. "You wear it well."

"Hey!" she laughed back, shaking her head as she tried to suppress a smile at his words. "Fine. I guess. All I wanted to say is, don't sweat it about your past."

"Why would I?"

"Because it's the same for everyone when they first become reapers. It's not like we don't regret things. We do." Alisha's mood sobered, and she nodded over towards the makeshift room divider, towards her bed. "I have a younger sister. She was only ten when I left, and not seeing her grow up is the greatest regret of my life. She's at university now, and I couldn't be prouder of her, even if I'll never see her again."

She paused before wagging her finger in the air

for Ryder to wait, darting over towards her corner of the room and reappearing with something in her hands. Handing the scrappy photograph over to Ryder with a shrug, she continued, "This is her."

Taking the offered image, he scanned the face of the young girl with the same fiery hair as her older sister, beaming out from a summer garden. He passed the photo back, emotion hurting his chest. "She's cute. Looks really happy there."

"It was when we were kids, before I starting doing stupid stuff. We were happy." Alisha gave a sigh, scrutinising the photo as though to burn the details into her mind, before pocketing it and gazing back up at Ryder with bloodshot eyes. "But it's okay, because I know she's okay. And every time I help someone who has a sister…I know what to say to them, I know how to comfort them. Being a reaper has allowed me to make up in some way for what I've done." Seeing Ryder's sad look as he gazed down at the threadbare carpet, she added, "It'll come, in time. Just keep going, and you'll find your redemption. Good to have you here, Ryder."

As she turned on her heel, making her way out of the room to go downstairs, Ryder stared after her with a mixture of wistfulness and longing. He let out a huff, yanking his jacket off and placing it on the bed next to Gabe's, throwing himself down onto it and letting his face fall into his hands. *I want redemption. So badly. So many in here have lost so much more than me. Maybe I was wrong.* Wiping his hands down his face, he raised hopeful eyes to the sunlight streaming through the window behind his bed. *There were so many things I blamed on anything and anyone else but me…but it was me all along. I could have changed my life at any point, and I didn't. Well, now I can. I'll be the best reaper anyone's ever known.*

Truly smiling inside for the first time since the unfortunate crash so many nights ago, Ryder laid back on the bed with his arms linked behind his head, his heart lightening at the thought of how good the next hundred years would be, compared to the previous twenty-eight.

CHAPTER SIX

Ryder glanced down at his phone for the tenth time. His next collection had already come in, and he was ready for it. The back-lit screen of the phone offered up no helpful suggestions, which he really needed —as it had merely led him to outside the General Hospital by staying lit until he reached it. The tattoo had given its usual burning signal every time he had to turn a corner, and Ryder was fast getting used to the twitch of instinct his insides gave during his journey. *At least as I'm down here, I don't have to go through that fucking portal. Unfortunately, even I know there's got to be hundreds of people in there waiting to pass over. How do I know which is mine?*

Pulling his collar up high, Ryder heaved his chest with a deep breath, marching forwards and gliding through the revolving doors as though he were made of mist when no one appeared to be looking. Landing on the other side in the foyer, he took a moment to search the sea of faces milling in and out of the hospital and through the corridors. There were nurses and receptionists all babbling incoherently to one another over the semi-circular desk in the centre of the space. Everything was crisp white and modern glass, sun streaming through in ribbons of yellow happiness. It was cast across the faces of several elderly patients in wheelchairs, all chatting to one another or staring peacefully out of the window, as their respective nurses or relatives moaned about life in general and took turns having cigarette breaks. A single green fern grew in a pot on the desk, drooping as though it hadn't been fed for many days. Ryder gave a chuckle. If the plant was anything to go by, he wouldn't have wanted to come here for treatment.

Following his gut, he sauntered along the large speckled tiles below his feet, halting in front of the large directions map. Tracing his finger over the coloured routes, he gave a low gasp as his stomach gave a twinge over the word *'Paediatrics'*. The idea of having to collect a child made him nervous, but if it had to be done, he figured it had to be done. Readying himself, he made his way through the hospital, weaving through corridors and hallways to his destination.

Elizabeth Davies clasped little Thomas' hand firmly, as though the extra effort of touch might just snap him out of his endless sleep. Tossing her tousled blonde hair over one shoulder, she squeezed her eyelids tightly together, preventing the flood of tears that lay behind them. Opening them again, she smiled down at her son, his curling, sandy-brown hair surrounding his tiny head like a halo, his mouth puckered into a rosebud as he slept.

Damn this leukaemia. If only he had hadn't got worse. Elizabeth wasn't stupid. She knew Thomas wasn't going to get better, not now, but she wished her little guy would at least wake up. Catching a cold had been the last straw for his fragile, six-year-old body, and he had slipped into a coma two months ago. It had been frightening, going to tuck him in and finding him so cold, his breathing laboured. Her days and nights since then had melted into one long, continuous round of doctors and hospital stay-overs. She was lucky enough that the hospital had set up a room for her here, for the reason — as they so delicately put it — Thomas was on the edge of 'not waking up'. She had no job to break up the string of days, her job had been as her son's carer when he got really ill.

Elizabeth tucked the long skirt of her blue, flower-printed dress around her legs, suddenly aware of a cold draught breezing through. Her deep green eyes roved around the room, as though she might find the source of the cool air, but she was met only with the sullen beeps and ticks of the respiratory equipment. A shiver running down her spine, she reached over to pull the woollen coverlet up Thomas' small frame, pausing to stoke a hand gently over his pale cheek.

Her chest clenched to see him laid so still, tiny tubes running from his nostrils, dark eyelashes trailing his puffy cheeks. She would have given anything at that moment to see him flash his big green pools of eyes at her, a reflection of her own. His hair was his father's —not that she thought about him that much.

A flash of anger ignited inside, and she couldn't hold back the hot tears that welled this time, brushing them away roughly. *Thomas' father was an arsehole. Thank the gods he doesn't take after him.* Thomas' father, Robert, had been her husband, once. As soon as he found out she was pregnant, he had done a runner. Apparently, he hadn't been 'ready' for a child, so she was left on her own, changing dirty nappies and soothing Thomas' teething cries while holding down a job. But she had her parents to help her, and she was grateful for that. Elizabeth smiled to herself as the thought of her own mum and dad came to her, and it soothed the tide of fury roiling in her stomach. They didn't know about Thomas, though. They knew he was ill, but they didn't know he had slipped into a coma. Every morning, Elizabeth would wake up with every intention of ringing them and asking them to make the two-hundred-mile journey to see him, but each time she tried, she would replace the receiver before the beeps even gave out. Ringing them to see him would be like admitting...that he was going to die.

Easing back into the green plastic of the hospital chair, she let out a heavy sigh, sinking her face into her hands. She wouldn't have admitted it to anyone, but inside, she was crumbling piece by piece. Every day seemed like another weight around her neck, and there was no one else to talk to about it. The nurses tried, and she was grateful they gave a damn, but it wasn't the same as having one person she could really confide in. Raising her blotchy face up again, she stemmed the tears once and for all, giving a loud sniff as she reached to her large bag for a tissue. *Come on, Eliza. It won't do any good if Thomas wakes up and sees you bawling by his bedside. Stiff upper lip, girl.*

Even the sound of his name in her head was like a ray of golden sunshine, and she scrubbed at her nose with the wrinkled tissue as she reached over again, taking his tiny hand in her palm. "Oh, Thomas. Come back to me."

This was the spot. He could feel it. The tattoo burned like a snakebite. Ryder glanced through the glass partition into the Children's Ward, peering around at the myriad of children and teenagers all playing or chatting around the main area. *I can't just wander in there. I don't know if I believe no one can see me, whatever Greek said. I'm going to need some sort of cover-up.*

Biting his lip, he spun around to check the corridor, tapping a finger thoughtfully against his chin. A small room was just off to the left, and he could glimpse a few lockers. The carefully stencilled letters above the door spelt out *'Changing Room – Doctors Only'*. Making sure no one was watching him, Ryder slunk along the wall and slipped inside the changing room, hearing no one moving about within. Quickly snapping one of the lockers open, he snatched up a long white doctor's coat, shrugging his leather jacket off and donning the doctor's overcoat instead. Deciding whether or not to leave his jacket, he plumped instead for simply carrying it under his arm, as though he was on his way home.

After checking there was still no one about, he passed through to the corridor, careful to close the locker again, and stood in front of the glass partition doors. Licking his lips, he concentrated hard, and sank through like it was mist. Greek had let him know that he could concentrate on solid handles and move them if he wanted, but it was easier to sail through when no one could see him. To his relief, he found Greek had been right as well about being seen, and no one looked up as he entered, save for a few of the children. Ryder wondered if those who were close to death could perhaps feel something off him, but he forgot about it as they busied themselves once more in Lego or dolls, and he sauntered past them as though he had made the trip a thousand times.

It's somewhere along here...yes, the private rooms. Here. His gut led him past the main play area, past the medical desk, and through into a quiet hallway. There were four doors on either side, all of them marked with signs for privacy. Ryder let his hand go out to touch the trim along the walls, trailing them over the rough paint until he halted outside the second door. His tattoo gave a final sear of fire, and he knew he had the right room. Ryder's heart picked up three-fold, and he tugged unconsciously at the collar of his t-shirt, a sudden need for air gripping him. This was going to be even harder than Abigail, he knew it.

Focussing hard, he gently pushed down on the door lever, popping it open with a soft click and letting a crack of light through. From where he stood, he could make out a small child laid on the bed, still as death, tubes all over his body leading to complicated-looking machines. Ryder closed his eyes shut for a second, needing to stop himself from running away from the private room. It hurt his heart to see the pitiful boy lying there with pale skin, no flush of youth colouring his cheeks. A woman was seated by the boy's side on a green plastic chair, but Ryder couldn't see her face. A cloud of blond hair, tousled and long, fell down her back in waves, over the summery, bohemian dress she wore long to her ankles. Her hand was closed around the child's, and Ryder could hear the sniffles of her preventing herself from crying.

As he hovered in the doorway, she spoke softly to the boy. "Oh, Thomas. Come back to me." Her voice cracked on a sob, and a tissue was produced from her other hand, wrinkled from earlier use. "I need you, little man. You're all I really have in the world. The most important person in my life." Her golden head bent, and she whispered, "Don't leave me."

I can't hang about eavesdropping. Time to get on with it. Clearing his throat loudly, almost dramatically so, Ryder swept the door open in a rush and stepped into the room, hoping she wouldn't notice. *Wait—what the hell are you doing? She can't see you anyway.* For a second, the cardinal rule floated around his head, but he brushed it away angrily.

The woman looked up towards him with glassy green eyes, her anguish reflected in their depths, and she sniffed loudly as she forced a smile onto her face.

Hurriedly scrubbing at her face, she gave a hollow laugh. "Sorry, doctor, I didn't see you there. Don't mind me."

Doctor? Oh, shit...she can see me. What the hell? Frozen to the spot, Ryder opened and closed his mouth like a goldfish gasping for air. His pulse became a livewire again, drying his throat with panic. The woman continued staring at him questioningly without looking away, raising her eyebrows and offering a sad smile when he didn't make any sound. Snapping his mouth closed, Ryder managed a wry smile, brightly replying, "Please, it's fine. It's okay to be upset." *I don't understand this. How can she see me? Greek has some explaining to do. I can't take the boy while she's here though. Hell, maybe I can console her a bit. Ankou and Morrigan wouldn't mind that, right?*

"Maybe, but I know I need to keep my spirits up, too." Rising up sharply, the woman held a hand out, scrunching the worn tissue tightly in her other hand like a comfort blanket. "I don't think I've seen you here before. New, yes? I'm Elizabeth Davies, Thomas' mother."

"I'm, er...Doctor Thompson. Yeah, I'm new. I'm...sorry about your little boy." *Thank fuck I've got a common surname.*

Elizabeth cocked her head, shrugging her shoulders. "Thanks. He's going to be okay though. I know it." Another nervous laugh. "I know you guys say otherwise, but...I know my little man. He doesn't give up without a fight." She gazed down at the still child for a moment, her lip wobbling, before she burst into tears once more.

"Oh! Mrs Davies, please sit down," Ryder gushed, racing to her side. Forgetting for a second that he had to concentrate his energies, his hand slipped through the small of her back, but she didn't seem to notice. Charging himself, he placed his hand around her shoulders, helping her sit down as he moved his palm to rub small circles on her back. Crouching down, he smiled up into her tear-streaked face, suddenly taken by how much more beautiful she was up close. Tiny freckles dotted her nose and cheeks, and her lips were so pink they were almost blushing. "You're right," he agreed vehemently. Regardless of his mission, he had to give her some hope. At least at this moment. It wouldn't be right to take that away from her. "It doesn't matter what we say. We're often wrong, you know."

"Yeah?" Elizabeth asked, hope lighting her features for a moment.

Reaching over to squeeze her hand, Ryder whispered, "Yeah. So you hang onto that. Thomas will wake up, you'll see." *What the fuck are you doing, Ryder? Grim Reaper, remember? You're meant to take him to the Otherworld, not tell her he might wake up.* He gazed up at the hope shining in her eyes, and he collapsed under her stare. *Fuck it. Maybe he will wake up. Maybe Ankou and Morrigan are wrong about him.* Ryder glanced around the room, frowning as he noted a ghostly figure of the little boy wasn't anywhere in the room. *After all...he's not floating around like Abigail was. Shit, that's it. He's not going to die. Surely.* It was the only explanation. Why else wouldn't he be here? Although in his heart of hearts, Ryder knew it probably meant nothing, he couldn't take Thomas away from Elizabeth just yet. Not when she was so broken. It knew how it felt.

CHAPTER SEVEN

"So how did you get on? Did you find your collection okay?"

Ryder quietly drew a sharp breath at Gabe's question, checking himself before clearing his throat, and answering casually, "No, couldn't find whoever it was. I'll look again tomorrow."

"Ah, no worries," Gabe grinned, jerking his head into the pool club. "Lots of us have a couple of those at times. Sometimes it can be a few weeks before we find them. Where did it lead you?" Leaning against the grime-covered brick wall, he flicked his lighter, pausing to light the cigarette hanging from the corner of his mouth. Inhaling deeply, he blew out a plume of smoke as he wagged his finger in understanding. "I bet it was the hospital. It's always the hospital."

Fearing that Gabe knew more than he was letting on, Ryder pulled his leather jacket closer. "How did you know?"

Gabe let out a booming laugh, his emerald eyes twinkling. "It's always the hospital when you can't find someone. It usually means it's someone in a coma, so they're not gone just yet, but they're on the threshold." His mood sobered, and he sucked in another calming breath of the toxic smoke.

Ryder's pulse thudded against his neck with relief, and he relaxed his shoulders, giving a curt nod. "That makes sense. But...er...don't any of them ever wake up? I mean, if they're not gone yet, there's a chance, right?"

Fixing Ryder with a curious narrowing of his eyes, Gabe let another blue tower of smoke drift from the corner of his lips. "I've never known it. But I suppose it could. Ankou and Morrigan are usually never wrong, though."

"I guess," Ryder replied in an easy tone, forcing a grin onto his face. "I just wondered. I've still got a lot to learn about all this."

Gabe's expression eased back into calm, and he nodded profusely, reaching across to slap Ryder's shoulder. "It's alright, mate, you'll pick it up. Better that you ask questions now than later."

Leaning against the other side of the doorway, Ryder folded his arms over his chest and gazed up towards the night sky. It was a clear night, unfettered by clouds and wind, revealing the silvery disc of the moon. This far out of the city, the streetlamps and car headlights did nothing to diminish the glittering carpet of stars, and Ryder could actually see most of them for the first time in his life. Letting out a sigh, he drank the sight in, a deep, inner calm washing over him. "Hey, Gabe?"

"Yeah?"

"How did you end up here? Or is it a secret?"

There was an uncomfortable clearing of Gabe's throat, and he shuffled his feet against the tarmac. "No, it's not a secret. I'm just guarded, same as you. But I can tell you. You won't like it though." Another stringent plume of smoke filtered through the night air. "I killed my wife and daughter."

Ryder's breath caught in his lungs, and he snapped upright, staring at Gabe's relaxed figure with dread. He hadn't expected that. "You...murdered them?"

Gabe shook his head slowly, not meeting Ryder's intense gaze. "No, I didn't say that. I didn't murder them. But they did die because of me. I didn't like to say. after what you said about your father."

"Drink?"

"Yeah. I liked a good drink. I mean, the hard stuff. Add a hard life, and you've got yourself a toxic cocktail."

"And yet you still drink beer and smoke cigarettes."

That time, Gabe did twist to fix his stern glare on Ryder. "I don't drink like I did then. I never will again. But they help to numb the pain. I know it's not right, but show me someone who does everything right." Letting out a harsh breath, he threw the end of the cigarette to the ground, stubbing it out as he ground his shoe against it. "I had a good job, nice house, beautiful wife and daughter. I loved them more than my own life. When I lost my job, due to the company making cutbacks, I went off the rails. That's when I took to drinking. One night, my wife — Lucy — tried to leave with Harriet — that's my daughter — and I stopped them. I don't even know what I was thinking." He paused, running a hand over his slicked-back hair. "I got in the car, locked the doors, and we got into an argument. I was pissed out of my skull, and not watching where I was going. We skidded off the road on the bridge — you know the big one, the one that leads out of the city? The car went into the water, and...we all drowned at the same time. Oh gods, I'll never forget Lucy's face when they left me in the Hall of Rest. They couldn't run away fast enough. And little Harriet. She kept shouting for me as her mother carried her off." He ended his tale on a broken sob, clearing his throat loudly again.

"Fuck. I'm sorry, Gabe." Ryder's words were spoken with genuine pain, his face darkening at the torment the man before him went through. "That can't be easy, but...it was an accident."

"That's what everyone says. But it still plays on my mind that I was drunk. Maybe it wouldn't have happened if I wasn't."

Clarity shining through his mind like a searchlight, Ryder strode over, laying a hand on Gabe's shoulder. The taller man looked up in surprise, he eyes clouded with memories, giving a cursory glance at the hand. "Look, Gabe," Ryder began uncertainly. *This might be taken the wrong way, but maybe it needs to be said.* "I know it's never going to help heal it, but maybe there was a reason for it."

"Reason?" Gabe snarled, knocking the friendly arm away and clenching his fists. "What fucking reason could there be for such a gorgeous little girl to be taken away from life, from her friends, from those who loved her? From her father?"

Holding his hands up in defence, Ryder gave a hard swallow, stepping away nervously. He could take Gabe if he had to, but getting into a fight wasn't what he planned on doing, he liked the guy. "I didn't mean it like that. Hear me out. I'm not saying it was fair, or that it was right, just that there was a *reason*. Maybe you were meant to become a reaper all along. Maybe they went onto an even better life, you know? Where...I don't know...Harriet is a princess or something."

Gabe continued glaring at Ryder for a moment, slowly uncurling his fists as he let out a resigned breath, falling back against the wall. "Maybe. I hope so. I have to hope that. I know you didn't mean anything by it, sorry. It still hurts so much, though." He gave a short laugh. "Maybe it's meant to."

"I can't believe that," Ryder interrupted, his

words firm. "It'll happen one day. Just not yet."

The air between them thinned from the built-up tension, filtering away to nothing as Gabe smiled back at Ryder. He tilted his head against the bricks, closing his eyelids slowly as he took in a deep breath. "Thanks, Ryder. I needed someone to say it." Jabbing his thumb towards the door, he added, "I think this lot are scared of me."

"Just for the record," Ryder grinned back, "I'm a little scared of you. I'd give it a go, but I wouldn't want to be on the wrong side of your fists, know what I mean?"

The two men chuckled as they made their way over to the door, Gabe slapping a hand heavily on Ryder's back, making him cough. They disappeared inside, closing the door over with the loose glass rattling in its frame.

As the street outside fell into silence, only broken by the odd faraway police siren or dog howling to the moon, something moved in the shadows. Across the street, previously unseen by the two reapers, a black figure garbled to itself in an ancient language. Before it could be noticed by a watchful eye, it slipped around the corner and vanished into the alleyway beyond, jumping over bins and boxes as though the devil was on its tail.

Ryder stared up at the ceiling with his fingers latched over his chest, listening to the steady breathing of the others. Someone gave a gentle snore, mumbling to themselves before the bed creaked with the weight of them turning over, falling asleep once more. Tapping his thumbs together, he tried to stop counting the cracks in the plaster, slamming his eyelids closed and forcing himself to drift off.

His mind was too clouded with troubled thoughts about Elizabeth and her son, Thomas. *I should just do what I've been asked to do, wait for Thomas to appear in the room, and take him to the Hall of Rest. Death happens. It can't be prevented. Why is this one so difficult for me? It's not like you know them personally. And yet...there's something about Elizabeth. About both of them. Like I'm supposed to know them.* Ryder fidgeted to his side, staring across the empty half of the room, his cheek pressing into the cool fabric of his pillow. Letting out a sigh, he shook his head to himself. *I can't do it. What if he's not supposed to go? Even Gabe admitted—to a point—that it might be a mistake. What if he's meant to wake up, and I take him anyway? Then I'll have to live with his mother being heartbroken, and knowing I took him when he could have had a good life anyway.*

"Shit," he muttered to himself, sitting up as quietly as he could manage. Sitting on the edge of the mattress, he rubbed his hands through his messed up hair and down his face, as if he could wipe away his insomnia. Only dressed in his boxers, he reached over for his t-shirt, pulling it over his head before tip-toeing across the patchy carpeted floor to the landing. Giving a backwards glance to be satisfied the others were still fast asleep, he edged along to the stairs, crouching down them to avoid making them creak.

As he entered the main living area, he halted, heart thudding in his ears as he squinted into the darkness at the figure sat on a sofa. As he scanned the distance to his stun gun, left on one of the tables, the figure twisted their head towards him. "Hey, Ryder."

Breathing out in relief, his temples throbbing from the sudden race of his pulse, Ryder padded into the room with bare feet. "Hey, Alisha. I thought you were asleep."

She leaned over to switch the nearby lamp on, its cheap plastic dome of a lightshade coming to life with a dull yellow glow, illuminating her face in sharp relief. Alisha's legs were curled up beneath her faded pyjama bottoms, her normally svelte hair stuck at odd angles around her face, as though she had been tossing and turning in bed. Waving towards Ryder, he noticed a large bottle of vodka in her hand, no glasses in sight.

Raising an eyebrow at the bottle, he asked, "Got enough for a spare glass?"

"Sure," she nodded in return, pointing over towards the kitchen area. "There's some glasses in the bottom cupboard. Knock yourself out."

Squeezing past the over-stuffed sofa, Ryder passed through to the kitchen area, banging cupboards open and shut until he found a relatively clean tumbler. Shuffling back through, he took the offered bottle from Alisha's hand and poured himself a large slug of the crystal liquid, before plumping down on the opposite sofa. Knocking a gulp of the vodka back, he let out a hiss as it burned his throat, leaning back to survey his companion. "Couldn't sleep either, huh?"

Alisha shrugged, drawing her feet closer to herself as she lifted the bottle to her lips. Shutting her eyes and giving a shiver at the sharpness of the vodka, she wheezed, "No. My head won't let me."

"I know what you mean," Ryder murmured, letting his finger toy around the rim of the glass, staring down into the bottom of the drink.

"Why?"

He raised his icy blue eyes to her question, wondering how much to tell her. After a moment's hesitation, he replied, "Nothing really. Just trying to sort things out in my head. About death."

"Oh...that." She nodded knowingly, her fiery hair bobbing like flames around her small face as she took another swallow of alcohol. A few drops landed on her oversized hoodie, and she brushed at them absentmindedly, adding, "Same here. I wonder sometimes...how do they know?"

"Who?"

"Morrigan and Ankou. How do they know who to take? What about when we have to wait a few days for someone to go?"

A pang of fear crept into Ryder's nerves, and he cleared his throat, burying the sound in his drink as he took another mouthful. *Does she know?* Casting aside his doubts, he cautiously answered, "I don't know. I suppose it's a kind of sixth sense. I mean, they're in charge of it all."

Alisha huffed, leaning her head back against the torn fabric. "I guess. But I sometimes wonder if..."

"If what?"

"If when death is near, death comes, you know?"

"Death comes? I've no idea what you're talking about. You've lost me, Alisha."

Shuffling on the sofa so she could lean forwards, Alisha gestured earnestly with her hand, swaying a little as she moved. "It's like that saying—if a tree falls in the forest, does it make a sound?" Alisha jabbed her finger in the air to make her point, quenching more vodka. "If death doesn't come in the room...does death come? If we never turned up, maybe some people wouldn't die. Not the ones who are ready, but the ones who don't show up right away."

Ryder narrowed his eyes at her, her discernment just a little too insightful. "Have you been speaking to Gabe?"

Alisha's brow furrowed at his words, shaking

her head profusely as she slurred, "No. Why? What's Gabe got to do with it?"

"Nothing. Forget I mentioned him." Swilling the alcohol in his glass before downing it and finishing it off, Ryder rose from the sofa, clanking his tumbler onto the cheap coffee table. "You've given me a lot to think about, Alisha. I'm off to bed though. Goodnight."

"G'night," she replied merrily, raising the bottle in a salute as she reached across for the TV remote, clearly settling in for the night. Ryder gave a tense smile, waving back before striding over towards the stairs.

The first rosy bars of morning peeped through the cracks in the windows as he trudged across the bedroom, sinking into his bed with a heavy sigh. Pulling the cover high up over his head, Ryder squeezed his eyes shut and tried to force himself to sleep for a few hours. But the image of a green-eyed, blonde-haired angel and her son stayed behind his eyelids.

CHAPTER EIGHT

Elizabeth glanced up as the young doctor made his way in, still with a leather jacket under his arm, just as he had been last time. He grinned at her broadly, and she nearly melted under his crystalline gaze. She might have been thinking about Thomas more than anything else, but she was only human, and the guy was one fine specimen.

"How is he?" Doctor Thompson—as he had introduced himself last time—asked softly, leaning across the bed to regard Thomas with concern in his gaze. "Any better?"

"A little," she replied happily, beaming across at her son. "The nurse said his eyelids twitched last night. I mean, they said it could just be a reflex, but it's more movement than he's made for weeks now." As if by instinct, her hand came up to play with her necklace, a short length of colourful plastic beads Thomas had made for her. She never took it off. It was like a link to him, even when he was in the coma.

Doctor Thompson perched himself on the edge of the bed, heaving a sigh as he nodded. "That's good. That's really good."

Her brow furrowed as she peered around to the base of the bed, eyeing the doctor curiously. Pointing an ivory finger at the boards hooked over the footboard, she asked cautiously, "You can check his charts. You know they're only there? It's just that's the first thing you guys normally do."

"Oh, er...of course," he gushed, sliding off the mattress and snatching the clipboard up, rifling through it furiously. "Yes, I can, er…I can see he's improved a little." Gently placing the red plastic folder back onto its holder, he gave a chuckle, his broad shoulders relaxing. "I'm sorry. I'm new. I still forget the simplest thing."

"Oh, that's fine. I've seen much older doctors than you come in here and forget to look too," Elizabeth winked back, wrapping the rainbow of beads around her fingers as she leaned back in her seat, crossing her legs beneath her floaty gypsy skirt. "Are you a Paediatrician then?"

"No…er…I work in the ER."

"Oh." She wrinkled her nose in confusion, her heart fluttering for a second with unreasonable panic. "Then…may I ask what you're doing here?"

Doctor Thompson's smile fell, and his cheeks flushed with colour as he stammered, "Well, I was passing through to see one of the other doctors, and he happened to mention something about Thomas. I just wanted to see if I could help. In any way. In you know what I mean."

Elizabeth softened at his blushing, holding back the giggle in her throat as she waited for his eyes to meet hers again. The flutter of dread melted away when she saw the honesty in his eyes. "I do. Thank you. And it's nice to have you here. You seem to talk to me like a real person. The other doctors are nice, but they all talk to me as though they're afraid I'll burst into tears. Which I know I did when you last saw me," she laughed merrily, "but you didn't look nervous and try to talk about medical jargon. You made me feel better."

Doctor Thompson shrugged, placing his jacket down onto the bed. "What else could I do? It was the right thing to do."

There was a lull between them for a few moments, only broken by the hiss and click of the respiratory machine, which had become both a soothing and irritating sound for her all at once. Reaching down into her beaded shoulder bag on the floor by her feet, Elizabeth produced a bag of sweets, pulling one out and offering the bag over to Doctor Thompson. "Want one?"

He looked as though he was going to reach over and take one, his hand coming out to the bag, before he retracted it with a shake of his head. "Sorry, I'm trying to cut down on my sugar."

"No problem. I like having some nearby, just in case Thomas wakes up." She gestured to the bag with an apologetic grin. "Jelly Babies. I'm always telling him not to eat too many, but he loves them."

"Yeah? I loved those as a kid," the doctor replied, chuckling to himself. "Thomas has good taste."

"Can I ask you something personal?"

"Of course. Anything."

"What's your first name? I feel like...I feel like I should call you 'doctor', but it doesn't feel right. You're too friendly to be 'Doctor Thompson'."

He broke into that dazzling smile again, flashing an even set of teeth at her. "Thanks, I guess. My name's Ryder."

"Ryder." Elizabeth sat back again as she looked him over, chewing slowly on the sweet jelly in her mouth. "It's a good name. I like it."

"I like yours. Elizabeth. It suits you."

Elizabeth bit her lip at the way he rolled her name across his tongue, glancing over at Thomas so she could hide the red creeping over her cheeks and forehead. *I think the cute doctor is flirting with you, Elizabeth! But...it's not the right time. Not right now. When Thomas wakes up.* Clearing her throat, she gazed back over her willowy shoulder towards Ryder, asking, "Do you have any children?"

Ryder paced across the room to grab another chair, plonking it down on the other side of the bed before seating himself heavily, shaking his head at her question. "No. I didn't even have any younger brothers or sisters. Wish I did though." His tone was wistful, as though there was some hidden secret he wasn't yet willing to share with her.

Not wishing to pry further as she realised he was hiding something private, Elizabeth jerked her head towards the sandy-haired child lying on the bed. "You know what else he loves? Dinosaurs."

Ryder leaned forwards, raising his eyebrows. "Yeah?"

"Oh, yeah." Elizabeth grasped Thomas' hand again, stroking it as she roved her eyes over his gently rising and falling chest. "Anything with dinosaurs, he's got to have it. Pyjamas, toys, bedsheets...you name it. You know Jurassic Park?"

"Who doesn't?"

"I didn't want him to watch that film until he was older, I thought it would be too scary. But...he saw it at a friend's, now he wants it on all the time." Turning to chuckle at Ryder, she raised her spare hand in a *who-knows-why* gesture with her open palm. "Turns out, he cheers the T-Rex on. Every time."

Ryder burst out into a fit of infectious laughter, relaxing into his seat. "He's a cool kid. Is that what he wants to go into when he's older? You know, dinosaurs? I don't know the term for it."

"A palaeontologist? Yes, that's what he wants to do."

Ryder's face sobered, and he linked his hands together, resting them on the base of the mattress. Tapping one finger nervously against his other hand, he asked quietly, "And what about you? What do you normally do?"

The question made her freeze for a second, and she tossed over what to say in her mind, her throat drying up. This was the bit where she got to point out just how dull she was. Thomas was her life. Everything. There was no time for herself, what with his illness. Taking in a deep breath, she tilted her head to peer over at Ryder's earnest face staring back at her. "This. Thomas has been in and out of hospital since he was a baby. His...er...his father's not around, so it's just me and my little man. It's a lot of work, so I don't really get time to myself. When I need to let off some steam, I make jewellery for myself. I guess that's pretty lame, huh? Thomas made this for me though." She brought her hand up to her throat again, hooking her fingers beneath the necklace and bringing it up into the light so that Ryder could see it properly.

He rose up gingerly, easing his way around the foot of the bed, bending down to inspect the necklace carefully. "It's not lame at all. It's a cool thing, being able to do something creative. I don't have a creative bone in my body, I can't even draw a stickman. And the necklace is beautiful. It's a good luck charm, I'm sure."

When he was this close, Elizabeth could see the ring of cool grey that surrounded his sea blue irises, and how the light glinted off his jet-black hair, making it appear to shimmer like a crow's feathers. Musky, warm, male scent washed over her, and she bit back an inaudible gasp at his presence, wondering how it would feel to bury herself in the rough stubble that lined his firm jaw. Snapping back to reality as he straightened himself, she let the necklace fall back into place around her neck, unfolding and folding her legs beneath the purple skirt, suddenly feeling underdressed in her simple sandals and bohemian outfit.

As though he had sensed her uncertainty, Ryder cleared his throat loudly, striding back over to his chair. She chewed on her lip for a moment, deliberating over something, and Ryder stared at her with interest as he twisted back to her. "Ryder...can I ask you a weird question?"

He raised an eyebrow and pressed his lips together in a bemused smile. "Sure, I guess. Depends how weird it is."

"Well, you might not like it, so tell me if you don't." Ryder made his way to the chair and lowered himself into it, pyramiding his hands together as he leaned his chin on them. Elizabeth ran a tongue over her lips nervously, her grass-green eyes never blinking as she added. "It's about...intuition, that sort of thing."

Ryder laughed merrily, easing his shoulders back. "Why would I mind that kind of question?"

Elizabeth looked away, glancing over at Thomas. "Because it's kind of about death too."

"Ah." He sobered instantly, following her line of sight before roving his eyes across her earnest expression. "That's okay too," he answered carefully. Elizabeth's fingers knotted together at his answer, as she wondered if she might need tissues again. Eyeballs prickling, she blinked hard, willing herself to stop.

"Okay, well my question was this. Have you ever felt like you just *knew* something? Kind of like gut instinct, but for something that wouldn't necessarily be a survival instinct."

Ryder nodded slowly. "Yeah, I've felt something like that. At times. You'll have to be more specific though."

Elizabeth swallowed hard. She hadn't mentioned this to anyone before. *Why am I telling him? I barely know him. But maybe that's why it's easier.* "Okay. Well, this will sound strange, but here goes. I've always...I've always been able to 'know' things. I knew when I was a kid that an old lady had passed away in my room, because I used to see her in my dreams. I knew when I was a teenager that my mum would get sick—she got better, by the way. When I was pregnant, I was so happy to have my little Thomas, but I just *knew* he would be ill somehow. I felt it, long before he was born. And," she finished hesitantly, "I felt it the night he got worse." Glancing back up at Ryder with a self-conscious grin, she added, "You probably think I'm mad."

His expression blank, Ryder shook his head and waved his hand for her to carry on. "Not at all. Trust me, you're preaching to the choir. Go on. How did you know?"

Taking a deep breath, Elizabeth reached down to pull the folds of her skirt loose, puckering them from their deep creases. She wrapped a loose thread around her index finger and snapped it free, casting it aside to the floor with a sigh. "I'd drifted off in the living room, taking a nap. Thomas was upstairs in bed, but he had a bit of a cold. I was having this dream about playing with him in the garden, then suddenly he was gone." She shivered, reliving the memory with startling clarity. "I looked everywhere, but couldn't find him. I woke up straight away, and I knew I had to go upstairs to check on him. He was running a high temperature, and his sheets were soaked in sweat. I called the ambulance straight away and tried to wake him up, but he'd already fallen into the coma."

Ryder cleared his throat, breaking the silence

that fell after she finished speaking. His voice was hoarse as he rasped, "I'm sorry, Elizabeth. But at least you went to find him when you did. Whatever it was, it woke you up and made you go to him."

Forcing a smile onto her lips, Elizabeth nodded profusely in response. "Exactly, that's what I tell myself. If I'd gone up just an hour later..." She trailed off, squeezing her eyes tightly before opening them again hurriedly, shining with unshed tears. "Well, I didn't, so I won't think about that. There's something else too."

"What's that?"

She blushed, her heart fluttering as she wondered whether or not to tell him. "I felt it before you came in, you know. It's probably coincidence, really. But I had this dream about a doctor with black hair coming to see me. Only...the weird thing was, he turned out not to be a doctor at all." Elizabeth laughed, a little too high and forced. "Obviously that bit isn't true, but still."

Ryder grinned back at her, but it didn't reach his eyes this time. Elizabeth's laugh died as she saw something akin to uncertainty in his gaze, and she swallowed back her shyness. *I knew I shouldn't have told him. I just feel so comfortable around him.*

He eased himself up from the chair, reaching back to scoop his jacket up and make his way over towards the door. "It's no coincidence, I'm sure of it. I'm glad to be here." He smiled over at her, the uncertainty vanishing in the wake of his natural charm breezing through again. "I've taken up enough of your time, Elizabeth, sorry. I've got to, er...get going." He waved his jacket apologetically, emphasising his reason for the sudden departure.

"I hope I didn't scare you off!" she joked, hoping she didn't sound too desperate. Her hands clenched up unbidden, and perspiration formed under her warm fingers at the tight hold on her skirt.

Spinning back around, Ryder shook his head firmly, placing his hand kindly on her shoulder and squeezing it. "I promise you haven't scared me off at all. Nothing you could say would do that. I just noticed the time, that's all. I'm running late."

"It was good seeing you though," she added hurriedly, sudden worry gripping her that he might take her guarded demeanour as a reason she didn't want him them. "Please come back whenever you like. Like I said earlier…I feel like I can talk to you."

Ryder flicked his tongue out over his lips, glancing over towards Thomas. As he surveyed the small child laid out on the pillow, he gave a firm nod. "I'll definitely be back. I'll see you next time, Elizabeth."

And with that, he was gone. Elizabeth stared at the pale wooden door for several minutes after Ryder had left, clutching Thomas' hand tightly. It didn't feel right to flirt while he lay so quiet and still on his hospital bed, but she meant what she said. It had been good to talk to someone who didn't treat her like she was a moron who didn't understand medical terms. Someone who had just…talked to her. About Thomas. Like he was awake, not asleep. Unable to think more on everything without bringing her sadness to the fore, Elizabeth popped another jelly baby past her lips and chewed slowly, reaching over for the TV remote. She needed dull, everyday life to wash over her at the moment and drown her, make everything else go away for a while.

Ryder stormed through the hospital corridors in

a rage with himself, the doctor's coat tucked discreetly beneath the biker jacket on his arm. Stabbing a hand through his hair, he punched into a nearby wall as he strode past, pushing all of his focus into it. *What are you fucking doing? Why? Why are you doing this to yourself? And to her?*

When he had leaned over her, it had been like summer breezing into his grey, miserable life. Her sweet, flowery scent, carrying all the promises of sunshine and warmth, her mane of golden hair so soft he could have sank into it and been happy to never resurface. The way her neck arched gracefully into her slim shoulders, her tinkling laughter, her sparkling emerald eyes. *No, emeralds aren't deep enough. More like absinthe.*

As he burst out through the main doors of the hospital, fresh air slammed into him, and he breathed it in gratefully. It soaked into his lungs, bringing him the clarity he so desperately needed. Setting off at a steady pace along the pavement to the carpark, where his gleaming motorbike was parked, he tried to remember why he was here. But Thomas was improving. There was no way he could take him yet. Not if he would live. *Ankou and Morrigan must have got it wrong. Just this once. He's not going to die. I just need to wait until he wakes up, then I can let them know.*

Bracing himself against the railing that surrounded the carpark, the two coats still clutched in his fist, Ryder bent his head and blew out a heavy breath. *I have to wait, anyway. I know I'm not supposed to speak to anyone, but if Thomas lives, I don't ever have to see Elizabeth again. I just leave them, and go on to my next collection.* Even as he twisted around to hop onto the seat of his Ducati, shrugging the leather jacket on as he stuffed the doctor's coat under his shirt, Ryder knew it wouldn't be that easy.

He wanted to see Elizabeth again already. She was getting under his skin in a way no woman he had ever known before had.

CHAPTER NINE

When he arrived back at the pool club, the mouth-watering scent of spices hit his nostrils, hurrying his descent from the bike into the building. As he made his way over, he turned sharply, catching a glimpse of something out of the corner of his eye. The evening air was rich with the curry cooking inside, and the lack of streetlights offered no assistance in picking something out from the shadows. Twisting slowly, Ryder scanned the nearby structures, his palm hovering over the stun gun at his back. Nothing but the stiff wind met him, a single plastic bag merrily dancing its way down the road.

Shrugging to himself after a few more seconds of searching, he moved his hand, making his way over to the front door. Gliding through, the sounds of laughter and loud voices enveloped him, bringing a sense of coming home. As he paused in the doorway, Gabe, Alisha and Mika glanced up and smiled at him. "Come on in, Ryder," Gabe called from the far end, a long pool cue in his hand as he waved him in. "How's things?"

"Good. As always," Ryder shouted back, forcing a grin onto his face. "What's the smell?"

"Dinner," Mika spoke up, flicking back her long black hair. "Devin and Drew are making curry."

Ryder's stomach rumbled at the mention of the delicious food being prepared, and he strode across to the refrigerator, yanking it open to grab a cold beer. "Damn, I haven't had curry for ages. Can't wait."

Mika's eyes never left his figure as he came around to perch on a sofa arm, popping the cap off his bottle. She shifted her position, moving her long legs as she propped her chin on her hand, her expression emotionless as she asked, "How's the collection going? Did you find them today?"

Giving a quick glance over to Gabe, Ryder nodded before taking a mouthful of the refreshing liquid in his hand. *Guess he told them.* "Yeah, I found them. All done and dusted." He had already made the decision to lie on the way over. The way he saw it, the other Reapers would only keep asking, and if they found out what he was really doing, they would try to talk him out of it. And he couldn't allow that. For Thomas' sake.

Mika leaned back, clearly satisfied with his answer, and leaned back to peer towards the kitchen before turning to face him again. "It's for the best. You'll get into the swing of it soon. Took me about two years before I could do it without worrying about the ones they left behind, but it got better."

Ryder's fingers clenched around the glass of the bottle, and he narrowed his eyes at her statement, cutting a little too close to the bone for comfort. The uncomfortable sensation that the others knew more than they were letting on crawled along his skin, and he was about to stand up and confront them, when McKenna burst in through the main entrance, breathing heavily. Her hair fell across her forehead in strands, and her chest rose and fell rapidly with her captured breaths, her stun gun hanging from one hand with a finger on the trigger.

"Guys, you need to come outside, *now*. I thought I saw a Warder."

The effect her words had was instantaneous. Gabe dropped the pool cue with a clatter, charging across the room and shoving past McKenna, his stun gun raised to his shoulder. Alisha and Mika weren't far behind, both women dropping to a crouch as they neared the door. Ryder was about to follow them, when Devin and Drew came out from the kitchen, beckoning him over to the back door. Moving quickly as he reached behind his back for his weapon, the three of them made their way through the bright yellow-tiled kitchen, the scent of mild curry tainting the air.

Crouching down in front, Drew ushered his brother and Ryder to follow suit, creaking the eggshell-painted back door open. He stared out into the night, eyes roving across the buildings as he knocked the lock off his gun with a practised movement of his thumb. "See anything?" he hissed.

"Not me," Devin whispered back, nudging Ryder as he glanced over his shoulder. "Ryder, you?"

"I don't even know what I'm looking for," Ryder murmured back, every muscle in his body tense and ready for flight. "What do they look like?"

"A shadow," Drew mumbled. "Not a regular shadow, it'll appear to be in the corner of your eye, then vanish again. They like being invisible, but you can always catch a glimpse of their forms before they run out of the way."

Ryder's blood froze to ice as he remembered his caution before entering the pool club. Pulling the stun gun clean of his belt, he cocked it and replied carefully, "Then I think I saw one. A few minutes ago, before I came in. I thought for a moment I saw something moving by the far buildings, then it was gone. I thought I imagined it."

"No, sounds like one of the Warders," Drew remarked grimly, his eyes locking onto Ryder's. "Reapers have a sixth sense for them. Show us where you saw it. It'll have moved by now, but it's somewhere to start."

Pushing past the twins, Ryder crouched along

the lino floor to outside, shivering as the cold night air made his body temperature drop. He put his hand out to the rough wall, the grit of the bricks scratching into his fingers as he moved alongside the building to view the alleyway down the side. All was still, no movement at all, and he came out further until he could see the carpark out front where the others were roving about, Devin and Drew close behind him. Pointing up to his left, he gave a nod, whispering, "That's where I saw it."

They came out from their hiding spot, straightening up to join the others, who had spotted their appearance and slowly made their way over. Gabe jerked his head towards the street to his right. "I saw you pointing over there. See anything?"

"Yeah, a few minutes before I came in. It vanished before I got a good look though," Ryder confirmed, his blue eyes hard with steel as he spun on his heel to get a better look at the towering structures surrounding the carpark, all glaring down with gaping eyes for windows. He took deliberate steps towards an alleyway directly opposite the pool club, narrowing his eyes as he zeroed in on an odd shape. For a moment, he thought it was nothing more than another black bin bag, haphazardly dumped by the side of a bin, but something about it didn't look...right. Ryder heard the clatter of footsteps as the others trailed after him, and he brought the stun gun up to line it with his sight, moving forwards into the darkness of the alley.

The bag...moved.

Without waiting to see what it would turn into, Ryder squeezed his finger against the trigger, aiming it straight for the creature that rose up. He didn't know what he expected from the weapon, but a blast of white energy burst from it, flying towards the dark creature like a lightning bolt. For a second as the flash burned into his retinas, Ryder thought he saw the twisted features of a demonic being with horns, its red eyes wide in horror as it darted out of the way of the energy. The unexpected force of the explosion thrust Ryder back, and he landed hard on the pavement with a grunt as Gabe pounded up alongside him and let out another deafening crash of energy at the Warder.

Before it could be caught again, it let out a screech, throwing its arms up and disappearing in a circle of white-hot flames it cast in its defence. The fire ricocheted outwards as it vanished and retreated to its realm, the heat burning Ryder's skin as he scrambled backwards out of the way, the flames lighting up the graffitied walls of the alley for a second. He blinked a few times, attempting to chase away the throbbing pain behind his eyeballs as the world slowly came back into focus. Gabe's hand came up behind him, gripping his arm and helping Ryder to his feet as he dusted himself off.

"You okay?" Gabe's voice was concerned, but gruff.

"I'm fine. Just didn't expect the gun to do that," Ryder admitted, doubling over as he breathed in deeply, resting his hands on his knees. "What the hell was that?"

"Just pure magical energies, forced through the barrel of a gun," Alisha replied merrily, slipping her own weapon back into her belt, her grey eyes shaded over with worry. "I don't know what's in it, and I've never wanted to. All I know is that the Warders are terrified of it, and they burn up if you catch one of them in it."

Ryder frowned, rising up carefully, putting a hand out to balance himself against the wall as he locked eyes with her. "So...not a stun gun?"

"Not really. More of a burn-them-all-to-Helheim

gun."

Gabe spun his weapon around on his index finger, casting a glance into the alleyway before fixing the others with a stern glare. "This is serious, guys. I've never known a Warder come this close before. Tonight, we're taking turns at keeping watch. I'm not going to wake up with a shadowy freak-show screeching over me. Let's face it, I need my beauty sleep."

CHAPTER TEN

Ryder rapped lightly on the door, peering in through the glass window to spy if Elizabeth was in there. She jerked her head up at the sound and broke into a brilliant smile, waving him in. This was the fourth time he had been this week, but still Thomas didn't appear in the room. He was certain now the little boy was getting better, and Ankou and Morrigan had got it wrong.

Swinging the door wide open with a squeak of the hinges, Ryder stepped inside with a large plastic bag in his hand, grinning conspiratorially. He chuckled at Elizabeth's curious frown, and reached into the carrier, pulling out a stuffed green dinosaur toy. "It's for Thomas," he explained with a smile. "I thought...well, I thought he might like it. And there's some Jelly Babies too," he gushed, reaching into the bag and producing the sweets, handing them across to her. When she didn't respond, simply staring down at the bag of sweets in her palm, sweat prickled on the back of his neck. "I'm sorry...should I not have got them?"

"No! No, it's not that." Elizabeth looked up at him with eyes glistening with tears, her nose wrinkling as she sniffed. "It's a lovely gesture. I just didn't expect it." She jumped up from her seat, waving her hands in front of her face in an effort to prevent herself from crying, sauntering over to the window. The sunlight caught the edges of her yellow sundress, making it appear as though she was glowing. "You're very kind. No one's come in to see and been so nice, I just..."

"Hey, come on!" Ryder ran across the room in a

flash, wrapping his arms around her before he had a chance to think about his actions. He froze, waiting for the moment she would scream because his arms had slid through her like a ghost, but his eyes widened in amazement as he glanced down and saw that he was hugging her. *Guess I'm getting better at this concentrating thing.* She twisted around in his arms, rubbing at her red eyes as she buried her face in his chest, sniffling as she halted her sobs. He leaned down to breathe in the scent of her hair, coconut filling his lungs as he pressed a hand against the nape of her neck. Rubbing his thumb over the velvety skin, Ryder bent down to her ear, whispering, "It's okay, Elizabeth. Don't cry. I just thought it would be nice, that's all."

She didn't respond, but she brought her palm up to press it against his chest, deliberately raising her glistening eyes to meet his, her lips parting as she let out a gasp. Her pea-green eyes roved across his face as her fingers trailed higher, sliding up into his hair and curling around a few strands as though hanging on for dear life. The touch of her hand was electric across his nerves, sending blood pooling into his groin and making his eyes flutter close at the touch.

Ankou's reminder floated through his head again. While he knew talking to Elizabeth was bad enough, there was no way he would allow them to do anything...more. Extricating himself reluctantly, Ryder squeezed her hands before letting them go, smiling in a friendly manner at her. Elizabeth seemed to check herself, clearing her throat and stepping away as she folded her arms over her chest. "I'm okay now," she confirmed, beaming back at him. "Just a momentary lapse of emotion. Would you like to put the dinosaur near his pillow? I'm sure he would appreciate seeing it when he...when he wakes up." Her sentence trailed away again, but she kept a straight face, gesturing towards Thomas.

"Sure, of course." Ryder snatched the stuffed toy up again from where it lay at the foot of the bed, taking a deep breath and shuffling closer to the little boy's head. He was as still as he had ever been, his chest rising and falling with the rhythmic beats that echoed off the walls, his curling fawn hair fanned out on the pillow. Taking the toy in one hand, Ryder gently placed it above Thomas' crown. *Where it can watch over him. In a way.* Letting out a sigh, Ryder put his hand on the frail child's shoulder, patting it comfortingly. "Please get better soon, little Thomas." There was an edge to his words that he hoped Elizabeth wouldn't catch, a hint of the turmoil inside.

Ryder tucked his hands into his pockets and chewed his lip for a moment, eyeing Elizabeth as he quietly said, "I'm going to go now. But…if you want anything…" He trailed off, realising it wasn't as though he could give her a phone number. "Well, I'll be around. I'll come see you both again."

Elizabeth looked up sharply, the peaceful serenity back on her features. "You don't have to go. Please."

Damn it. Her eyes…she could ask me to do anything and I'd crumble. Anything. But not this. Even his heartbeat seemed to pause as he glanced down at his boots, so out of place with the rest of his assemble. He was surprised Elizabeth hadn't mentioned it before now, but then, her mind wasn't on shoes. Shaking his head firmly, he repeated, "No, I've taken up enough of your time today. Sorry, Elizabeth, I've got things to—"

"Please, don't worry," she grinned back brightly, but her eyes lost their shine at his words. "I…I keep forgetting you're a doctor here. I'm probably keeping you from all kinds of important business."

"No, you're not," Ryder protested, rubbing a hand over his neck anxiously with a lopsided grin, but the smile never met his eyes. "I love coming to see you both, really. I promise I'll come back to see you tomorrow. I just wanted to give Thomas his dinosaur." His nerves tightened as he made the promise, but he knew he had to return anyway. But the more time that passed, the more he worried he would enter and find a ghostly Thomas stood by his own frail form.

"I understand. Then, I look forward to your visit tomorrow, Ryder," Elizabeth murmured back, giving a sly wink.

Ryder didn't return the wink as he left, but his chest clenched of the thought of leaving them both in the hospital room. All he wanted to do was charge back in and take them both somewhere else, wake Thomas up, and live happily ever after. *Shame shit like that doesn't happen.*

Ryder paused at the traffic lights, willing the warning red to change to amber as quickly as possible. Tapping his finger impatiently against the handlebars, he snarled below his breath as the lights resisted to his desire to get out of here as quickly as possible. A cloud of dark thoughts had settled in his brain, and the Friday night crowds were not helping, a need to drown himself in intoxicating liquids until his brain exploded taking over.

The scent of stale beer and cheap perfume filtered through the air from the bar opposite the lights, attacking his nostrils like stringent acid. *Fuck it. I need a drink.* Screeching his tyres as he spun the motorbike around sharply, ignoring the blaring horns from the cars behind, Ryder raised the beast over the pavement with a protesting growl. Pulling it as close to the front of the bar as he was able, he kicked the stand down and switched off the ignition, giving a resigned sigh as he sat for a moment. *Maybe I shouldn't do this. Old habits die hard.*

Gritting his teeth and pushing the sensible thought away, he jumped off the bike and made his way towards the loud heavy metal music and laughter drifting through the open door of the bar. Shrugging his collar high about his neck, Ryder dived inside, the evening darkness blinded by flashes of red fluorescent light. The music grew in intensity as he was swallowed up by the suffocating heat of the dive bar, pounding into the floor so hard his whole body vibrated in time to it.

As he made his way through to the main bar, he sidestepped a young couple in a dark corner, openly thrusting against each other in the throes of passion as though they were alone. Ryder gave a chuckle, shoving in past the crowd of sweating dancers to gain the attention of the barman with a wave as he leaned over the plastic bar-top, careful not to let his jacket get in any of the sticky drink spill. As the young barman with a half-shaved purple hairdo nodded over at him, Ryder shouted over the throbbing music, "Give me a bourbon. Something strong."

Waiting impatiently for his short as he tapped his fingers against the bar, Ryder twisted around to view the occupants of the nightclub. Every woman was dressed in torn-off shorts or mini-skirts that could double as belts, and the men looked suitably cheap in Adidas and Nike tracksuits. Not Ryder's sort of place, but it would do. *One drink…maybe two. Then I'm out of here, to pretend again that I'm doing my job well. So much for my promise.* Sighing, Ryder spun around as the barman slid the glass before him, slapping five quid down in return as he snatched it up for a refreshing gulp. The spicy warmth of his old friend Jack Daniels trickled down his throat, igniting his insides with fire.

But I'm not doing this because I want to do badly at this reaper thing. I just can't take someone who isn't ready to die. Fact. Ryder leant his elbow against the bar and peered out at the sea of people again. As he gazed across the crowd, two odd faces jumped out at him, and he narrowed his eyes, hoping he was seeing things.

Warders. In here. With people.

They moved slowly through the swaying compression of bodies, fighting their way over to an unoccupied table. In the dizzying flashes of light, Ryder could finally see their true appearance, like the one he had almost caught sight of back in the alleyway the previous night. Long, gnarled horns rose from their temples, faces covered in dry, cracked skin that resembled tree bark, pus-filled boils and lesions breaking out across their cheeks. Their eyes were devoid of irises and deep red, blood floating in a river of fire with their irritated glares at the human populace around them. One of them had long, clawed hands that dragged on the ground as he shuffled by, and the other Warder sported slime-coated tusks poking out from the corners of its mouth. Turning quickly to avoid detection as they squeezed past, Ryder buried his face in the glass of bourbon, his ribs aching from the punishment they took from his thudding heart.

They swept past with a wretched stink of dying mulch and rotten eggs, so strong that Ryder was shocked no one else seemed to notice. He glanced over his shoulder at their backs, and flashes of their disguises flickered over their bodies, images of two men in tracksuits with cropped dark hair. *I suppose that's what everyone else sees.* Bravery getting the better of him, he scooped up his glass and pushed through the crowd as calmly as possible, ducking into the dark shadows of the sides of the club. Ignoring the moans of couples getting better acquainted with their one-night stands, Ryder slid along the walls until he was in listening distance of the Warders and perched himself on the edge of a worn booth-seat, craning his head to hear better through the glittering pane of modern glass behind the seat, between himself and the two demonic creatures.

"So why are we meeting in here? They stink," the first Warder rasped, his voice sounding as though it were climbing over a mountain of grit before passing his crusted lips.

"Because none of the reapers will come in here. You know how they're warned not to mix amongst the humans if they can help it," his companion rasped in reply, the lighter tone almost feminine in its sound, although scratchy.

"Perhaps. Why did you want to see me?"

"Empusa has asked for you personally. You are to go with me, to collect a very special soul."

"Special? How special?"

"Empusa wants this one for herself. We are not to harm this one before bringing it to her."

Ryder's brow creased in concentration as he listened intently, waving a drunken woman away testily as she attempted to sidle over to talk to him. Rolling her eyes and shrugging, the woman staggered back to her friends, swallowed up into the gyrating crowd as she disappeared. Turning back to the Warders' conversation, he sipped the amber alcohol in his fist, his stomach lurching with unknown gut instinct. Something about them was very off, even if he wasn't sure yet what it was.

"Why should we do that?"

"As I said, Empusa *herself* has requested this

one." The voice was firm, almost threatening in its words.

"Fine, fine. Where do we need to go?"

"The hospital. It's not far from here, we can be there in twenty minutes."

Ryder's hand froze, and the blood drained from his body in a cold rush, his ice-blue eyes hardening. *It can't be...*

"Why hasn't it been picked up by a reaper? Don't they normally wait around for those ones?"

Silence for a second, followed by the whisper of fabric as one of them presumably gave a shrug. "I don't know. Sometimes they miss them, especially when they're coma victims. But we've been watching them, and there seems to be nothing amiss. They have a new reaper, but nothing more."

His chest heaved with held breaths as he realised they were speaking about him. The glass cracked in his palm, and Ryder glanced down at it with horror, realising he had gripped it so hard he had created a fine hair-line down the tumbler. Placing it onto the nearby table with a shaking hand, he perked up his ears again, waiting for the remainder of their conversation as bile rose into his throat.

"What does this one look like then?"

"A young boy. His mother has been with him, but she sleeps on a night. I have watched her in the darkness."

It's Thomas. They're talking about Thomas and Elizabeth. Ryder didn't need to hear any more. Being careful not to be spotted by the sickening creatures behind, he shoved through the crowd, not caring if he bumped into anyone or not. Breaking free of the crushing throng, he dived out into the freshness of the night air, racing across to his bike. Firing the ignition as it burst into life with an animalistic snarl, he didn't even wait for the kickstand to be moved, and it broke away with a loud snap as he pulled the handlebars towards the hospital and Thomas.

CHAPTER ELEVEN

Ryder charged off the bike as soon as it hit the tarmac, uncaring as the chrome fittings grinded to a halt as the motorbike slid to its side. Jumping free of it, he dropped into a sprint towards the hospital entrance, gliding through the glass and steel like mist. It was still lit up with bright lights, but the foyer was empty except for one receptionist, staring blindly at her computer screen as she pretended to work.

Paying her no attention, Ryder raced through the corridors and passageways in blind panic, glad that he remembered every twist and turn to Thomas' room like the back of his hand. His lungs burned with his effort, and his temples throbbed with pain as his pulse catapulted around his body. Reaching the cheerful painted giraffes and elephants that signalled the glass doors to the Children's Ward, Ryder sucked in a breath, feeling it scrape past his dry throat as he rounded the corner of the glass. Only night-lights were left on for the children, a dull orange glow that peeked from underneath curtains around beds, the toys and games looking strangely malicious in the pitch darkness.

Ryder flew down the corridor to Thomas' room, past the main station where two nurses were deep in whispered conversation. They never saw him as he ducked into the room, breathing a sigh of relief as he saw the small child still tucked into his bed, alone in the dark. *Elizabeth must be asleep somewhere else. I hate to take him away...but I can't let him go to Helheim. Those fuckers aren't getting him.* Ryder carded his heated fingers through sweat-drenched hair, pulling the strands back away from his face as he strode around the bed. His fingers played along the edges of the wires and plugs, knowing that if he pulled them, it might be enough to make Thomas' soul appear. He tightened his hold around them, taking hold of the young boy's hand as he prepared to yank them from the wall.

I can't do it. I can't kill him. Even for this. But maybe I can defend him.

His mind racing between his only two options, Ryder swore under his breath. There was only those two choices. Either pull Thomas' cords, to allow his soul to come away to the Hall of Rest, or take a chance that he would be able to overpower the Warders with his gun and the element of surprise. Ryder's slippery fingers came around to his back, reaching for the grip of the gun as he drew it out with a soft click, surveying the gleaming barrel with a tired gaze. With a sinking heart, he realised there was no way he could risk it. *What if I don't manage to hit them? There's two coming, not one—that I know of, that could be more. And if this 'Empusa' wants Thomas so badly, then she'll only send more. It'll never end. And why does she want Thomas, anyway?* It was a question he hadn't given himself time to think about, but it made the fine hairs rise on the back of his neck. Whatever she wanted Thomas for, it wasn't good news.

Bending over the frail boy, Ryder smoothed back the child's sandy hair, squeezing his tiny hand tightly. "I'm sorry, little guy, but you have to come with me. I've got no choice. But you'll be safe, and I'll make sure your mum is safe." Ryder's voice broke as he spoke about Elizabeth. He knew it would bring her world down around her shoulders, but it would mean Thomas was out of the grasp of the demonic Warders. Just as he was about to pull the first plug from the wall, he caught the sound of raised voices from down the corridor.

"Yeah, we'll just go in here."

"What's it for again?"

"He's being transferred, different treatments, you know."

"No problem. Second on your right."

Ryder's head spun as he recognised the rasping voice from the nightclub. *They're here.* Moving as fast as a shadow, he dropped Thomas' hand and made his way over to peer out the door, making sure to keep out of sight. The two foul Warders were speaking to the nurses at the station merrily, their horrific features sharpened by the harsh lighting. Images of paramedics flickered over their forms, and Ryder dived back inside the room, blood rushing through his ears. "Now or never. Do it," he said firmly to himself, taking a deep breath and pulling the cords free.

A dull beep went up from the machines, and the respiratory machine whined as it wound down from keeping its tiny patient alive. Thomas gave a wheezing choke, as though struggling for breath, and Ryder clenched his teeth as he held back pricks behind his eyeballs, the sight making pain stab through his soul at the knowledge this was what had to be done. Thundering footsteps came up the passage outside, and not even knowing if it would work, Ryder threw everything he had at the door, using all his concentration to keep it closed. Colour drained from Thomas' cheeks as someone rattled the door-handle, trying desperately to get in. Sweat poured down Ryder's forehead as he kept up the strain against the door, feeling a push of energy from the Warders behind it. They knew he was in there now, and they were doing everything they could to get in.

Just as he was about to give up hope, a shimmer of colour appeared before him, a small figure with tousled, sandy hair melting through the atmosphere like a TV tuning in. *Thomas!* The shimmering grew stronger, and the tiny form of Thomas in his T-Rex pyjamas turned to Ryder with a confused frown, his rosebud lips pulled down into a pout. "Where am I?" he demanded in a petulant tone.

"Come here, Thomas. It's going to be okay, give me your hand," Ryder insisted, holding his palm out towards the boy as he gave a grunt, his power weakening under the combined assaults of the Warders on the other side of the door.

"No! I want my mummy!" Thomas cried out, stamping his foot against the tiled floor. As he glanced towards the bed, he caught sight of his lifeless body, and his eyes widened as he let out a high-pitched cry.

"Sh! No, don't look!" Ryder shouted, thrusting his arm out to snatch the boy up. It wasn't how he wanted to take him, but he had no choice now. Just as he leaned forwards to catch Thomas around his waist, the door burst open—and a spiral of purple energy swirled in front of Ryder's eyes at the same time. To his horror, the pull of the energy yanked him away before he could grab hold of Thomas, sending him sailing towards the ceiling against his will. A cackle went up from the Warders as they surrounded Thomas, and the child's scream pierced the air with ear-splitting terror.

"FUCK! NO!" Ryder roared with anger, struggling against his bonds as he tried to break free of Ankou's hold, but it was no good. The tunnel of energy swallowed him up towards the sky, and the Warders disappeared from his sight, Thomas' scream ringing in his ears.

CHAPTER TWELVE

He was bounced out onto the hard floor, and his damp palms hit the coolness of the black marble, the energy spitting him out as though he were a piece of rubbish. Ryder jumped to his feet in alarm, spinning around and searching for a door he knew wasn't there. Twisting back sharply, running shaking hands through his hair, he was confronted with the towering figure of Ankou, ominous in his very silence.

"Please, Ankou, you have to let me go! There's a—"

"ENOUGH!" Ankou's voice boomed around the hall, echoing back in mocking tones as he slammed his great staff into the ground, cracking the marble with the force. His bony fingers curled tightly around the wooden stick, splintering it as he glared down at Ryder with burning white eyes. "I sent you to be a reaper, and I find out you have been *conversing* with a human! We told you of a soul to be collected several days ago, and still he has not appeared! Would you like to inform me of what you think you were doing?" His voice came out in a hiss as he leaned down to Ryder, seeming to grow larger with every passing second.

Ryder clenched his fists so tightly his nails dug into his palms, quivering with rage as he roared back, "There *was* no soul to collect. You sent me to kill a little boy—I didn't sign up for that!"

Ankou let out a growl, his hood falling back and revealing his drawn face, taut with fury. "I sent you to collect a soul. If you have to wait for them, so be it. But you must never speak to a human. *Never.*"

"Fuck you and fuck your rules," Ryder snarled in return, eyes bulging as he took a step forward, all fear gone in place of his worry for Thomas. "I need to get back. *Now.* You have no idea what you've done."

"What I've done? WHAT I'VE DONE? Boy, I'm going to send your pathetic soul to the bottom of Hades!" Ankou cried, raising his hands high above his head. Black tendrils whipped out from them, knitting together in a canopy across the ceiling, casting the Hall of Rest into thick darkness. Whispering voices eddied around Ryder as he spun in a panic, raising his hands, ready to defend himself.

"My love, calm yourself." The soothing tones of Morrigan floated through the canopy of darkness, a ripple of energy that dampened the burning fury emanating from Ankou and Ryder. The tendrils slowly withered away to mist, and Morrigan strode through, a crow flying ahead of her and cawing loudly before circling and landing on her shoulder. Ankou paused, bringing his arms down slowly as he let out a low breath, twisting to glance at his wife as she stepped between them both. "What is going on?"

"This *reaper*—and I use the term loosely—has broken our cardinal rule. He has spoken to a human. On many occasions."

Morrigan's dark eyes hardened, but she said nothing, tilting her chin at Ryder as she pursed her lips. "Ryder? Is this true?"

Something in her gaze made Ryder shiver more than Ankou's display of power, something ancient and cold that left him uncomfortable. Forcing himself to hold her glare, he nodded sharply, answering, "Yeah."

"Why?"

Ryder flicked his cool eyes between the pair, bracing himself for the barrage of fury once more. "Because...because I'm falling for her. I'm sorry. I know it was wrong. But her son was in a coma, and not yet gone, and now he's been taken by Warders, so—"

"Wait," Ankou interrupted, his booming tone softened by the concern in his voice as he raised his eyebrows. "The child's soul has gone to Helheim?"

"That's what I was trying to tell you," Ryder sighed, pleading with his wide-eyed gaze for the two guardians to understand, to let him return. "I was just about to grab hold of him when you pulled me back. They were there, and now they have him. I'm sorry I didn't bring him sooner. It's just..."

"Yes?"

"I wasn't sure he was going to die. He kept improving, and his mother was so hopeful. I thought...I thought you might have got this one wrong." Ryder's voice trailed off, and he stared down to the floor.

"Oh, Ryder," Morrigan cut through his dire thoughts, making him jump anxiously as she placed a gentle hand on his shoulder. "We were worried you had not carried out your duties because you were abandoning your post. We did not realise it was because you feared taking a life that was not to be taken." She glanced back over at Ankou with a furious glare, and he threw his hands up in defence, shrugging his bony shoulders.

Ryder peered back up at them withdrawn features, his breath catching in his chest as he asked, "Please, let me go back? I need to save him."

Ankou shook his head solemnly, gliding across the floor as he drew near, his long robe whispering along the marble with him as he let out a mournful sigh. "I'm sorry, Ryder. But even if you go back, the child is gone now. We are not allowed to set foot in Helheim, or we risk Empusa's wrath."

For the second time that night, Ryder felt his heart stop in pain. Shaking his head rapidly, he took a step back, managing, "No, you don't understand. You have to let me try, at least! I heard his scream when they caught him, and—"

"My word is final on this," Ankou warned, his wrinkles deepening as he frowned. "I am sorry I pulled you back when I did, Ryder. But there is nothing to be done once the Warders have a soul. Let this be a lesson for the future."

"No, but...I..." Ryder stammered, hyperventilating as the reality of the situation slammed into him, nearly felling him with the weight of it. *Thomas is gone. Elizabeth will be broken. And I have to sit back and watch it happen.* He collapsed to the floor as the guardians gave him one last sorrowful gaze before gliding back to their thrones, stabbing his fingers into his hair and wiping them over his face.

Greek watched the verbal battle take place between Ryder and the guardians, his heart going out to the young man sinking to the floor. A reminder of a similar event from hundreds of years ago passed through his mind, and he folded his arms over his stomach in a comforting manner in response. It had been much the same, a soul who was between the planes of life and death, and not yet ready to go.

Worse than that, it had been his only true love.

Worse than leaving the ancient world when he was still a young man, the world that was young when he left it, was leaving the one man who had been the shining light in his dark existence. Diokles was a warrior, a bronzed figure that looked as though he had been created by the gods as the most beautiful work of art their fingers could fashion. When Greek had seen him, their dark eyes had met, and he had known there and then he never wanted to gaze into anyone else's eyes in the same way ever again.

The Grecian nights had been heated with passion and love, the two men tumbling together in white Indian cotton as they drank wine and talked early into the morning about their lives ahead. Greek could still feel the soft press of Diokles' lips against his own, yielding and firm as he sank into his strong arms. Then he had gone to fight in the Grecian army...and he wasn't seen again.

Broken with his pain at never seeing the young man who had stolen his heart again, Greek had ended his life on the edge of his balcony, falling away into the rocks below his cliff-side house. Years later, after becoming a reaper, he was confronted with the bedside of a Greek soldier who had fallen in battle. He appeared as though dead, struck on the head with the blunt edge of a spear, yet still he breathed unaided. Greek had recognised Diokles in a heartbeat — it was the one face he could never forget, even when the very names of his people were no longer spoken of on humanity's lips. He had stayed by his lover's side for days, willing him to awaken, when the Warders had made their plans clear to take him.

Then Ankou had brought him back, forbidding him to go back and save Diokles from being brought to Helheim. It was a torture Greek had never forgotten, and he saw his own pain again now, etched into the pale features of Ryder.

And this time, he wasn't going to allow it.

Waiting until Ankou and Morrigan had retreated to their thrones, Greek raced out from under the arches towards Ryder, marching quickly. Keeping a jovial smile on his face, preparing himself for his usual overdramatic manner, he hooked an arm under the young reaper's shoulder. Dragging him up from the ground, he leaned into Ryder's ear, whispering, "Say nothing. Come with me. I will help you."

Ryder glanced at him in shock, his mouth falling open as the glacial gaze roved across the older reaper's face. Swallowing hard, he gave a nearly imperceptible nod, allowing himself to be marched along as Greek led him under the arches and through the passages to the training area. Greek's pulse hammered against his temples as he laid his hand at the small of Ryder's back, making contact with the crinkled leather as he pushed Ryder towards the portal.

Finally out of the guardians' earshot, Ryder hissed, "Greek, what are you doing?"

Greek fixed him with a mournful stare, striding over to the weapons rack as he firmly replied, "Something I wish I'd done years ago. Just trust me." Reaching toward the weapons rack, he grabbed a large silver gun, fondling it with a caring caress. Twisting back to Ryder, he held the handle out, giving a careless shrug. "I want you to take this. It's mine—it's a damn sight more powerful than the one you've got now."

"Greek...I can't take that," Ryder breathed, drinking in the sight of the carved wooden handle, topped with a silver barrel. It had been created some time in the eighteenth century, and Greek knew it could pull a punch like no other energy gun they owned.

"Here, I mean it. Take it. It's only a loan, mind — I want it back." He jerked the gun towards Ryder until the younger man grasped it reluctantly, tucking it by his hip as he gazed over at Greek. Reaching over for one more item, Greek passed an oval disc over as well, turning it so that the etched metal hit the light with a brilliant flash. "This too. It's a shield, but no normal shield. I don't know what you'll find in Helheim, but this will protect you from most of it."

Ryder reached out to take the curved work of art from Greek's outstretched hands, turning it over before sliding his arm through the leather straps at the back. The disc itself was set with moons and stars, and a proud soldier stood in the centre, surrounded by fallen enemies as he thrust his sword to the sky. "Greek, this is amazing." He raised an eyebrow as he peered up in uncertainty. "You're sure I can have this? I don't want to damage it."

Giving a sad smile, Greek nodded. "It cannot be damaged. Not that easily, anyway. It once belonged to a brave man, called Diokles. He was...he was very close to me, once. And he would want you to have it. That shield was designed to protect, and it can do more of its duty in Helheim than it can gathering dust here." Pacing over to the portal, he crouched down to tap his hand against it, bringing the collected energies it held to life as he touched it. "I can send you back through here, and hide you from Ankou and Morrigan—for a time. Get to Helheim, save the young boy, and get back. That's all I ask."

"I don't even know how to find Thomas once I'm there. Or how to find Helheim itself."

Greek gave a firm nod. "I know that too. You will need something of Thomas' to guide you, something he has owned for a long time. I don't know any other way, I'm sorry." Striding over, he placed a hand on Ryder's shoulder, staring earnestly into his tense features. "The most important tool you have as a reaper is your instinct.

Use it to guide you, to tell you where to go, what to do."

Ryder clapped his hand on Greek's, then thought better of it and hugged the older man to his chest in a manly embrace, releasing him with a broad smile. "Greek, you're a better friend to me than anyone was in my past life. Truly."

Feeling a lump forming in his throat, Greek threw his hands up and gave a careless laugh, more forced than he meant it to sound. "Now don't set me off, I'm not stocked with tissues in here. Go. Quickly, before they catch on to what we're doing. And Ryder?"

"Greek?"

"Get out of there in one piece, okay?"

CHAPTER THIRTEEN

It was Christmas, and little Thomas ran madly around the tree in circles, squealing at the top of his voice. Elizabeth laughed at his excitement, eagerly awaiting the moment he calmed down enough to start ripping the paper off his gifts. The gifts she had scrimped and saved for over the last year, gone without salon haircuts and new clothes for, gone without a car for. Her parents had helped, of course, but she used a little of her savings too. They were worth it, every last one of them.

"Are you going to see what Santa brought then?" she giggled, catching Thomas mid-flight in her arms as he grinned up at her, his tiny face full of cheeky fun.

"Yes! Let's look, Mummy, come on," he cried happily, his cheeks flushed with breathless elation as he wriggled free of her grasp, his hair sticking up and lines still pressed into his face from the wrinkles on his pillow. Sliding down in front of the stack of presents, he squeezed his hands together and clapped delightedly, waiting for Elizabeth to seat herself in her favourite armchair with a mug of tea in hand. "Which one first?"

"Hmm…that one," she announced, unable to stop her eyes shining as she pointed to the largest parcel, wrapped in merry blue paper with reindeer and snow flitting over it.

Reaching over for it, Thomas took no time at all in tearing the wrapping away, leaving it in torn shards around him on the beige carpet. It took him a few seconds to register the brightly-coloured pictures on the box he revealed, before his eyes widened as he gave a dramatic gasp. "Mummy! It's a robot dinosaur!"

"That's right," she chuckled, helping his tiny fingers

get the lid of the box open. "I told Santa you had been a really good boy this year, and he said you deserved it."

"Thank you!" Thomas giggled, leaping up and throwing his arms around her neck. Elizabeth closed her eyes and hugged him back, her heart overflowing with joy at his happiness. As she linked her arms around his back, the fleecy warmth of his pyjamas vanished from her touch, and she snapped her eyes open to see what had happened.

Thomas was gone.

"Darling? Where are you?" she called out, a note of hysteria lighting her tone. As she jumped up from the chair, her mug went crashing slowly to the ground and spilled across the carpet, but she barely noticed. Racing through her living room, she searched behind every nook and cranny, even in places that she knew he wouldn't fit. "Thomas? Please stop hiding now, you're scaring me!"

Elizabeth opened her eyelids wide with a horrified gasp, her lungs aching with a scream that wouldn't come. She sucked in air, propping herself up on her elbow as she leaned over the side of the narrow hospital bed, blinking to rid herself of the fog of sleep. As she waited for the nightmare to filter away like sea-mist, she pressed a hand to her hammering heart.

No, it's still there. Something is wrong.

She couldn't explain it, but something in her gut screamed at her to move, to get going. *It's Thomas. Oh please, Thomas, wait for me!* Without missing a beat, she snatched up her dressing gown and threw it on as she sprinted to the door, yanking it open with a squeak. Still foggy from sleep, Elizabeth raced along the ward to Thomas' room, her pulse making her head spin as she saw lights on in his room.

A nurse at the station tried to catch her as she

flew past, but Elizabeth tore her elbow away as she stared forwards with a grim expression, refusing to believe the worst. *No. He can't have. He hasn't. He isn't.* The room eddied and swayed as she crashed into Thomas' door, pushing it open with sweating palms. Stood around Thomas' bed were two doctors and three nurses, all with mournful sorrow in their eyes. One of the nurses came across to gently hold her back for a minute, but Elizabeth struggled to remove her grip, slapping her hard when she didn't let go. "Get lost! He's *my son!*" she screamed.

One of the doctors nodded, and the group of medical staff slowly parted, allowing her access to Thomas' side. She rounded the bed swiftly, running to Thomas' side. The first thing she noted was that there was no sound from the many machines in the room, a peaceful hum and beep of white noise in the background at all times. The second thing she noticed was how still her little boy was. Too still. No movement from his chest.

The ground fell away from her feet as she clutched the tiny, cold hand of her son, collapsing to the side of the bed as she stared at him. Her heart shattered in agony, and her mouth fell open, letting out the baneful cry of a wailing banshee as she willed him to live, even as she knew he was gone. "No, no, no, no…Thomas! Come back to me, Thomas! *You hear me! COME BACK TO ME!*" she sobbed, the scream coming free of her chest. The world around her turned to water as tears pushed past her eyelids, swallowing her in their grief. "No! You can't be gone, little man!" she cried out, dragging herself up to his side and pulling Thomas into her arms. Cold though he was, she could feel the softness of his hair against her breast, the press of his upturned nose. "How did this happen?" she bit out through trembling lips. "*HOW DID THIS HAPPEN? Answer me!*"

"Mrs Davies, two paramedics came to take him to another hospital for treatment. When they found him...they switched off the machines. It was too late, he was already gone."

"Fuck you," she rasped, glaring daggers at the doctor who had spoken. The young blonde-haired man balked under her stare and looked away, glancing at his colleagues for assistance. Elizabeth turned back to Thomas' still form, running shaking hands over his head as her shoulders heaved with the sobs breaking from her insides. Salty water trickling into her mouth, she added, "You should have fucking *found me!* I didn't know about him going to another hospital, nothing! You bastards."

One of the nurses tried to gently —although somewhat more gingerly than her colleague —prise her away, but Elizabeth clutched him harder. "Leave us!" she yelled, keeping her son tightly tucked into her embrace. Glancing up at one of the doctors, an older man with a greying moustache and beard, she begged tearfully, "Please. I need to be alone with him."

"Miss Davies, we're just worried that —"

"I'm not going to do anything stupid," she spat out bitterly, rocking Thomas to and fro in her arms. "Just *give us a moment.*"

The doctor hesitated for a moment, letting out a heavy breath, before nodding at his companions. Leaning down, he pressed a gnarled, comforting hand into her shoulder. "Mrs Davies, just let us know when you're ready. We'll be outside," he murmured.

Elizabeth gave a nod, not looking as he removed his palm and moved across the room to join the others outside. As she heard the door slide back into place with a shushing motion, Elizabeth's features crinkled, and she sobbed her soul out into the sweet, childlike scent of

Thomas' hair. "Oh, my little man. Why didn't you wait for me? Why didn't you wait for Mummy?" Her grief tumbled out of her with no end in sight, a black hole which she knew would never be filled again. She didn't want it to be filled again. The light in her life had been snuffed out, and she never wanted to come out of the perpetual darkness it left.

She was so deep in her anguish that she never noticed when a tall figure glided through the door soundlessly, standing patiently at the foot of Thomas' bed. When the figure gave a rough clearing of the throat, only then did she give a start and snap her head up. "I thought I asked to be left alone! I only — oh, sorry. It's you, Ryder." Elizabeth's shoulders shook as she let another baying cry free, wrapping her fingers tighter around her precious bundle. "He's gone, Ryder! He's gone!"

"I know," he rasped hoarsely, his mouth set in a firm line. "I'm so sorry, Elizabeth."

She shook her head rapidly, unable to form words again as water flooded down her cheeks. Ryder moved smoothly around the bed and crouched down in front of her, putting his arms out and cradling her and Thomas in his embrace. Elizabeth allowed herself to be held, burying her face in his shoulder as she gave a silent cry, her chest lurching with the effort. A scent flooded her nostrils, once she hadn't noticed the last time he had come. Pulling away sharply, she took in the sight of him in his leather jacket with a frown, the doctor's coat nowhere in sight.

Ryder placed his fingers under her chin, forcing her to look directly at his cool gaze, his blue eyes dark with his own anguish. "Listen to me, Elizabeth. What I'm about to tell you will sound unbelievable, but I *need* you to believe me. Thomas is not gone — not yet."

"What?" she breathed between sobs, blinking as she tried to understand his meaning. Everything in her head felt jumbled together, as though her thoughts were creeping through cotton wool and obscuring themselves from her. "I...I don't get what you mean."

Biting his lip as he let out a heavy sigh, Ryder let his hands fall away, swallowing so hard she saw his Adam's apple bob. "Thomas is not yet gone. There's a chance we can get him back, but you have to trust me — which I know is asking a hell of a lot. But it's the only chance we have."

"Not...gone?" she repeated doubtfully, allowing herself to finally look down at Thomas' serene face. Her thumb drifted over his closed eyelids, and she croaked, "But he's gone, Ryder. Dead. My little baby is dead." Her voice broke on another cry as she uttered the words, and she pressed Thomas back into her arms again.

"Only his soul is gone, Elizabeth. And I can get him back. But I need your help."

Her lips parted as she gained control once more of her stuttered breathing, raising her head cautiously to fix Ryder with a curious glare. *I don't know what he's talking about. This makes no sense. But nothing about Ryder has really made sense since I met him. I've never seen him with any other doctors. I mean...* A ray of hope, so small she dared to believe it existed, lit inside her soul, and she whispered, "Ryder...are you...are you..." her voice trailed away, and she nearly snorted at what she wanted to say. "Are you an angel?"

A wry smile ghosted over his lips, and he shook his head. "No. But...I'm not human. Please, let me help him. Let me help you. You *have* to trust me."

Elizabeth glanced from him back to Thomas. Just as she was about to tell him to get lost and leave her to her mourning, she felt a twinge in her guts. Her sixth sense had always proved right in the past, and it was pulling like crazy towards Ryder right now. She gazed deep into the sincerity in Ryder's eyes, seeing nothing but truth in their depths. *I must be mad. But what if...what if something weird is happening here, and my boy can come back to me? Any chance is a chance. I will take anything over nothing.* Breathing heavily, she brushed back Thomas' hair, replying, "I'm insane. Or we're both insane. But I'll do anything to bring my little boy back." Her hands tightened. "Anything. What do you need?"

Straightening himself up as his joints popped in protest, Ryder grated back, "Something he has had for years. I don't know...a toy, a favourite item of clothing, anything. As long as Thomas has had it for a long time."

Slowly standing up, Elizabeth nodded firmly, with Thomas still in her arms. "I know just the thing. Come on, it's at our house."

"Woah...you can't come with me," Ryder warned, holding his hands out to stop her moving. "Look, it's dangerous. I need to do this alone."

"Like hell," she snapped back, anger flaring and momentarily taking place of her mourning, hiking Thomas up onto her shoulder. "He's *my* son. I'm coming with you, wherever it is you need to go. You can't talk me out of it."

Ryder stared back at her with a dark expression, but she held his gaze, jutting her chin in defiance as silence fell. The tension thickened in the air, and Ryder relented, wiping a hand over his face. "Fine. But you have to do what I say, and you have to stick with me —whatever happens."

"Whatever happens. I don't even know what you're talking back, but I'll try anything." Elizabeth had always believed there was more to life than just death, and something in her soul told her she was right to go with Ryder, even if he was speaking gibberish.

"Right. Then we can't go out the way we came in. There's an exit at the end of the corridor, away from the nurses' station. If you put Thomas back—"

"No." Elizabeth squeezed her son harder, shaking her head vigorously in response. "He's coming with us. I'll leave him at home, in his bed. I'm not leaving him here. They'll put him somewhere and—"

"Okay." Ryder put a hand out and grabbed her palm, pulling her towards him with a soft smile. "I understand. We have to go *now* though."

Before she got a chance to reply, he yanked her forwards, and pulled the door open with care. Voices could be heard down the other end of the hallway, but they were far enough away to tell them that the doctors and nurses had retreated beyond the nurses' station. Keeping his arm wrapped around Elizabeth's waist, Ryder steered her towards the end of the corridor, running on silent feet as they charged for the exit doors.

Slamming through them, the pair found themselves in a cold, tiled staircase, leading both up and down into other parts of the hospital. Dull white lights flooded the way down from the walls, the plastic casings grimy with forgotten insects and dirt. Jerking his head towards the bottom, Ryder hissed, "Come on. Down."

They clattered down the steps, and Elizabeth was glad she had the sense before going to sleep to leave her shoes on. Not knowing when she would have to run to Thomas' room meant it had become normality after a short time, despite the fact she was clothed only in a dressing-gown and yellow nightie. She nearly fell as they rounded a set of stairs, and gave a yell, slipping forwards as she twisted to avoid hitting Thomas in her fall.

Ryder caught her at the last moment, putting her upright and gently taking Thomas from her arms. Shushing her protests, he dragged her along, whispering, "It's okay, I won't let go of him. We can run faster this way."

Never taking her eyes off the precious child over Ryder's shoulder, Elizabeth charged forwards behind him, both of them making their way to the bottom of the staircase until they came to a bright red fire exit. Ryder paused for a second, giving Elizabeth a worried glance. "Listen. I've got a bike out there, so that's what we're running for. Just follow me, and keep up. When we open this door, a siren is going to go off in this place, and it'll only take them a few minutes to find us if we don't move quickly. Got it?"

"Got it." She gave a nod to show she understood, and squeezed his hand tightly, her own palms slick with cold sweat. Her grief still weighed heavily in her chest, but adrenaline drove her for the moment, holding it for when she wasn't running for Thomas' life. Ryder took a deep breath, and shoved the door wide open as he pressed down on its safety bar, a wailing alarm immediately ringing through the air at a deafening pitch. They tumbled out into the darkness of night, the air rippling through her thin nightclothes as she pounded along the tarmac, still gripping Ryder's hand for dear life. The siren grew fainter as they raced along the carpark, the streetlights above casting them in a bright yellow glow as Elizabeth wheezed for breath, her lungs on fire.

Reaching a shining Ducati, half of its side scratched with grit and fresh wear, Ryder jabbed a finger towards it. "Get on. Now." He easily grasped the handlebars and swung his leg over the seat, still holding Thomas in the crook of his arm. Elizabeth followed suit, tucking her dressing-gown tight around her waist to avoid getting it caught in the wheels. He shifted Thomas to his front as though he were sat in front of him, and glanced over his shoulder, nodding towards him. "Wrap your hands around my waist, so you're holding him too. I can't steer this thing and hold you both."

Doing as he said, Elizabeth slid her arms around Ryder's slim waist, latching her hands tightly against Thomas' torso. It was a squeeze, but she knew there was no way she was letting go. She noticed a strange metal disc hanging from the back of the bike, a gleaming shield that looked as if it was made of silver, but she cast it from her mind. It wasn't important right now. All that mattered was getting Thomas back.

Ryder hit his foot down on the accelerator, and the bike roared into life, vibrating beneath her legs with a fierce thunder of power. He swerved the handles around, and the bike veered off across the carpark, picking up speed as he zipped between cars and pedestrians. Elizabeth sharply closed her mouth and eyes as grit flew in, hiding her face against Ryder's firm back. Having never been on a motorbike before, she had no idea what to expect, and the blast of wind and debris was like tiny razors biting into her bare skin. She clutched tightly at Thomas' front, and the three of them disappeared into the night along the dark city streets as they left the hospital and her grief behind.

CHAPTER FOURTEEN

It wasn't until Elizabeth had unlocked and safely passed through her own front door, with Ryder behind her and Thomas' body in her arms, that she allowed herself to breathe. The tears still pricked behind her eyeballs, but her trepidation held them back, her mind focussed on whatever lay ahead for the time being. Nodding at Ryder as she flicked the light switch on, she said tersely, "Give me a moment. I'll put him in bed, then we can get going."

She passed through her familiar hallway to Thomas' bedroom, cautiously sliding the door wide open. Easily making her way across the usual scattered trail of matchbox cars and Lego bricks, Elizabeth paused at the side of his small bed, hesitating. She didn't want to let go of him, even for a minute. Cradling his head to her bosom with one hand, she pressed a loving kiss into his hair, forcing herself to keep the dam up.

"It's only for a little longer, and he'll be awake," Ryder whispered from the doorway.

She spun around in alarm, flustered as she hadn't heard his approach. Gripping the bundle in her arms with increased urgency, she croaked, "I can't do it, Ryder. I can't leave him."

"You have to, Elizabeth. It's only for a little while." His tone was steady, but she could feel a sense of fear behind them.

Shaking her head firmly, she explained, "No. What if no one is here when he wakes up? I can't leave him alone, Ryder, please understand."

"Fuck." Ryder twisted around and leaned against the doorframe, pressing his fingers against his temples as he thought for a minute, letting out a heavy sigh. "Okay. Let me see what I can do." He reached into his pocket, and as the jacket shifted up above his waist, Elizabeth's eyes widened at the sight of a gun, just peeking over his waistband. Oblivious to what she had seen, Ryder brought the mobile phone into the light, punching in a few numbers before placing it against his ear. "Gabe? It's Ryder. Yeah, I'm…I guess I'm fine. Look, I need you guys to come to an address, all of you. Huh?" There was a pause for a moment, as someone on the other end spoke, then he added, "I know, I know. Please? I wouldn't ask if it wasn't necessary. I swear I'll explain when you get here. Finkle Street—just off the main road through the city. Look for a tall block of flats at the far end, Flat 14B. Sure. Thanks, mate. I owe you. See you when you get here."

He spun back around to face Elizabeth, smiling tensely. "I've got someone coming to help us, one of them can stay with Thomas. They'll be about half an hour, taking in the time to get across town." Taking in her drawn, pale features, he gave a frown and asked, "What's wrong?"

Elizabeth's heartbeat raced through her veins as she carefully placed Thomas in his bed before she spoke, drawing the quilt up to his neck. Laid so quietly, he looked as though he was merely asleep. Passing a hand over his forehead, she gulped loudly, and asked in a trembling voice, "Ryder…what are you?"

"What do you mean?"

Swivelling around, she pointed towards the living room and followed Ryder through as he complied, gritting her nerves. He paused by the sofa, drumming his fingers against the back as he raised his eyebrows at her.

Elizabeth nodded her head towards his belt. "What are you carrying a gun for? You're not an angel at all, are you?"

Silence grew heavy as Ryder chewed his lip, staring without blinking back at her, his chest rising and falling rapidly as his breathing sped up. Finally shaking his head, he glanced down away from her. "No," he admitted in a whisper.

"Then," she hissed, making her way carefully towards him, fear strengthening her tone, "what the hell are you? What have I let into my home?"

Running a hand through his hair, Ryder let out a tired sigh, jerking his head towards the cabinet in the corner. "You got alcohol in there? I need a drink if I'm going to tell you all this."

"Sure. Help yourself," Elizabeth uttered with narrowed eyes, skirting him as he breezed past, bending down and rummaging through her cheap glasses and bottles. Seating herself heavily in the armchair at the far end, she reached across for the heavy iron poker hanging by her gas fireplace. It was only decorative, but she was sure it would still cause a nasty bump if Ryder tried anything.

He came back over to stand by the window, gazing out at the night as he poured himself a large slug of supermarket-brand whiskey. Knocking it back in one go, he licked his lips, peering down at her with dark eyes. "First off...no, I'm not a doctor. I'm not human, either."

"You said as much back at the hospital," Elizabeth conceded, bringing the poker up into her lap. He gave it a nervous glance, but said nothing. "But whatever you are, good people don't carry guns around in their belt."

"They do if they have to defend themselves from

the bad guys," he pointed out, pouring another glass. "I'm a reaper."

"Reaper?" Alarm bells sounded off in Elizabeth's head, and her knuckles turned white as she gripped the weapon in her hands tighter. "Like the *Grim* Reaper?"

"No...well, yes, sort of. I...oh, fuck, this is going to sound worse than it is."

"Anyone ever tell you that you swear too much?"

"Yeah, actually. An old lady."

"Well, she was right." Standing up sharply, her jaw clicked as she nodded towards him. "Go on."

Ryder leaned against the windowsill, being careful not to move the position of any of the many photos arranged along it as he placed the glass down and took to the bottle instead, clamping his mouth around the neck of the whiskey and taking a swallow. "I'm a reaper. It means that...I collect the souls of those who have died. I take them onto a place called the Hall of Rest —a good place— where they pass onto their next life."

There it was. The very reason he had been there in the first place. Every nerve snapped in Elizabeth's body, and fury lit up her eyes as she marched towards him, brandishing the poker as she screamed, "You were there to take *Thomas!* And you pretended to be my friend, and —"

"No!" He cried back, catching her wrists just as she swung the iron pole at his head. It caught him on the side of his jaw, and he hissed in pain, rubbing it against his shoulder. "Look, it wasn't like that. I *am* your friend!"

Fireworks exploded in her head as she drew away from him, the now familiar sensation of dizziness washing over her. She gave a harsh gasp, clutching for the back of the armchair as the world spun. *All this time...that's why he was there. That's why he never came in with anyone else. All along, Ryder was there for my son.* Ryder came up behind to catch her before she fell, but she righted herself, shoving him away so hard that he stumbled backwards with a bewildered expression. "Stay away from me, you monster!" she cried, throwing the poker towards him. Ryder dodged it at the last minute, and the iron bar went flying past his shoulder, crashing into the large mirror above the fireplace. It shattered into pieces like glimmering diamonds, falling to the ground in a cascade of glass.

"Look, listen to me—"

"No! I won't listen to anything else you have to say! I'm going to—"

"Please, Elizabeth!" As she tried to dart around him and get to Thomas, Ryder caught her arms and pinned her against him, twisting her so she faced him. Clasping her upper arms with a steel grip, he fixed her with burning glacier eyes, his face pale but solemn. "Listen to me. I didn't *want* to take him. Why do you think I kept coming back?"

"Because you're sick, that's why!" she sobbed, hammering her fists against his chest as she struggled to free herself from his hold.

Ryder let out a sigh, gazing down at her attempts as though she was simply a kitten batting at him with soft paws. Shaking her gently until she stared up at him with wide, tear-stained eyes, he rasped, "No. Because when I saw you both, I couldn't do it. Not to Thomas, and not to you. But...I should have. He's been taken by...by someone else, and I need to get him back so he's safe."

Halting her sobs, Elizabeth gritted her teeth and whispered, "Who has him? Who has my little boy?" A chill shuddered down her spine.

Ryder gazed over the top of her head for a moment, as if he was avoiding the question. "Warders. Reapers take souls to the Hall of Rest, where they get to go onto their next life. Warders take souls to their own domain, where souls are...look, I can't tell you this." His voice cracked.

Jabbing a finger furiously into his face, Elizabeth steadied herself, clenching her jaw as she retorted, "You tell me *now*. He's *my* son. Where is he?"

"A place called Helheim—not the same as the 'Hell' you're thinking of. That place doesn't exist. Empusa, Queen of Helheim, wants him for some reason." Cold determination shone in his eyes. "I'm not going to let that happen." Clasping her hands tightly as he spoke, Ryder leaned down to her, sincerity ringing true in his tone. "I mean it, Elizabeth. This isn't a 'maybe' thing. I'm getting Thomas back."

Staring up into his features, Elizabeth studied him for a moment. Her heart clamoured against her chest, making it pinch in agony as she tried to make sense of the situation. *He's a reaper. Come to collect my son. But he couldn't do it. So he's a good guy. Because of Thomas. And me. I hope...I mean, he's never lied to me before. Other than the fact he was a reaper, and I guess that wouldn't have been a great introduction.* Her chin trembling, she whispered, "This Hall of Rest...is it a good place?"

Ryder nodded firmly, relaxing his hold. "Yes. I went there when I died. It's how I became a reaper. He'll be happy, Elizabeth, I swear."

"And you promise you'll look after him?"

Fierce pride flashed in his expression as he pulled her closer to him, his lips mere inches from hers. "I swear, Elizabeth. Nothing in my life meant anything until I died and found you and Thomas. Now I'll do anything to protect you both."

Elizabeth's breath rolled out to meet his as she arched herself upwards, loosening his grip as her hands slid up along his firm chest towards his hair. Something caught in her breath, and her mind clouded over with thoughts of nothing but burying herself in his musky scent. *How can I be thinking of this. Right now? But it's like...like I'm being pulled to him. I need something, anything, to drown out my emotion right now. Just one kiss...*

A muscle ticked in Ryder's jaw as she moved, and he hoarsely begged, "Elizabeth, don't do this." His eyes shone with undisguised need though, and she could feel the same pull from him as she felt in her body, an ache screaming to be soothed.

Stabbing her fingers into his tousled hair, she closed the distance between them, the heat from his mouth sending nerve endings into spiralling cataclysm as her core ached for him. *He's a reaper. He's a reaper, Elizabeth. Don't do it.* But something told her it was right. She was still furious with him —but not for what he was, because he hadn't told her. *But how could he? Would I have done the same in his position? He didn't have a choice. And yet, he made one. For Thomas and me. And he's still doing it now.* Everything in her body throbbed for his touch, ached for his hands tracing along her skin.

Sensing her thoughts, Ryder tried to pull back gently, breathing hard. "Elizabeth," he warned, "you're still upset. I don't want to take advantage, okay? Please."

"I need this," she argued, her insides twisting in agony between her grief and her need. "I need to feel, just for a moment. Just for a moment." Before he could draw away again, she fisted her hands in his air and yanked him down, fastening her lips over his. A soft moan escaped her as she allowed herself to melt into his touch, even as he hesitated against her mouth. The moan seemed to snap him towards her, and he wrapped his arms around her, using one hand to clasp her nape, grunting as he relented and gave her what she searched for. She tentatively explored his mouth, their tongues dancing together as they clung to each other.

The kiss grew more urgent as Ryder twisted her around, slamming her up against the wall. Two framed pictures hanging from it wobbled and fell to the floor, the glass cracking as it hit the ground below. She gasped with need, sliding her leg up against his thigh. Catching it with a firm hand as he ravaged her mouth, Ryder pressed into her, grinding against her centre as she arched herself against his hard body. Thoughts and fears cascaded into the back of her mind as she lost herself in him, searching for the place that would fill the gaping hole left in her heart, digging her nails into his scalp as their teeth clashed with the violent passion of their lips meeting.

Dragging himself away, breathing hard, Ryder fixed her with cool eyes as he gasped, "No more. Not yet. We have to get Thomas back."

"Yes...yes, we do," she murmured in reply, using a shaking hand to wipe strands of hair away from her eyes as she nodded. The icy ache of anguish at Thomas being gone returned, and she bit her lip, holding it back as she tried to clear her mind for the journey ahead. "So, where do we need to go?"

"To Helheim. We'll go in, get Thomas' soul back, and take it from there." Ryder cracked his neck from side to side as he reached behind and pulled out a black gun, handing it across with a raised eyebrow. "It shoots energy, not bullets. I know it sounds weird, but it works, trust me. It's for the Warders, in case they attack. I'm still not happy about you coming, but if you are, you need to take this."

"I'm coming, Ryder," she confirmed, sending him a chilling glare. This was something she couldn't be moved on. It wasn't that she doubted Ryder's abilities. There was no way she would stand by while her son was in danger though. "Let me go and get his baby blanket — it's what you can use to track him. He's had it since he was a baby, I brought him home from the hospital in it. That is what you wanted, yes?"

"Please."

As he watched her retreating figure disappear into the darkness of her bedroom, Ryder blew out a harsh breath, shaking his head as he sank back onto the arm of the sofa. *What the hell just happened?* He understood it, even if it confused him. Elizabeth was grieving, and if kissing him made her feel braver about what they were going to do, so be it. The taste of her lingered on his lips, coconut and strawberries perfuming his mouth with her loveliness. No one else would ever be enough for him, not now.

Reaching to his side, Ryder felt for the silver gun Greek had trusted him with, admiring the sheen on the soft metal as he squeezed it tightly in his grasp. Thomas came back into his thoughts, the memory of the little child crying out as the Warders descended upon him. Closing his eyes shut, Ryder clamped his hands into fists, chasing away the horrific remembrance. *We're going to get him back. After that...I don't know. I really don't.* He was planning something. He didn't know if it would work, and it would mean appealing to the better nature of Ankou and Morrigan, but —

A loud bang at the door made him glance up in

alarm, cocking the safety off the gun in his hands as he rose from the sofa, pointing it towards the door. Elizabeth poked her head around the edge of her door in a fresh change of clothes, face drawn with worry, and he waved her back as he edged his way towards the sound. It came again, a louder thudding this time, as if someone was hammering their fists against it.

CHAPTER FIFTEEN

"Come on, Ryder. It's fucking cold out here!"

Recognising the sharp tones of Alisha behind the door, Ryder let out a relieved groan and raced across, letting the gun hang loosely in his grip. Pulling the latches back, he swung the barrier open to reveal the other reapers, all kitted out to the eyeballs with stun guns and various other weapons.

Gabe was the first one to rush inside, his gun held up and ready for a fight, jerking his head for the others to follow him in. As they trotted in, looking as out of place as a clown in a church, Gabe glanced over his shoulder at the shards of glass on the floor and back at Ryder with a hard glare. "Alright, Ryder. What's this about?"

Ryder nearly buckled at his friend's tone, already nervous with how difficult a conversation this was going to be. Licking his lips, he decided to bite the bullet, and started, "You know how I asked about the whole 'coma patients' thing a few days ago? Well, I know I was supposed to wait for the soul, then take it, but I couldn't."

"We guessed that," Mika piped up with a gentle smile, toying with a strand of her hair as she surveyed him with her dark hazel eyes. "We were waiting for you to tell us."

"You mean..." Ryder trailed off, a sense of betrayal flying through him like wildfire as he spat, "So which one of you told Ankou?"

Gabe's brow furrowed, and he straightened his spine, carelessly placing the gun in the holster by his side.

"What do you mean?"

Gritting his teeth to hold back the rage boiling inside, Ryder roved his eyes over his six companions, narrowing his eyes at each one. "Somehow, Ankou knew what had happened. He brought me back —just as the little boy was taken by Warders."

Gasps went up from the woman, and Gabe stepped forward with concern in his expression, his mouth planted in a firm line. "Woah, slow down, mate. Warders? Little boy? You mean the soul you had to collect was a child? Shit, we didn't know. That's hard." At Ryder's incredulous snort, he continued, "Look, however Ankou knew, he didn't hear it from us. I swear. Ryder...we don't do that to one another. You're one of us, our brother." Gabe appealed to him, holding his hand out in a show of solidarity.

Ryder's glare softened as he took in Gabe's solemn features, his voice ringing with nothing but truth. Giving a hard shrug, he clasped his friend's outstretched hand tightly. "Fine. It doesn't matter, anyway. I didn't want to take Thomas, he seemed like he was waking up. But I left it too late, and now the Warders have him. We have to go and get him back from Helheim."

A soft clearing of a throat came from the far end of the living room, and all heads moved as one to take in the sight of Elizabeth, stood with a blanket clutched in her arms. Raising her eyebrows at Ryder, she nodded over to the others, asking tensely, "Are you going to introduce me?"

As the other reapers stared on with gaping mouths, Ryder skirted the sofa to Elizabeth's side, wrapping an arm around her shoulders. Facing their disapproving gazes, he rasped, "These...are the other reapers. Guys, this is Elizabeth, Thomas' mother."

Alisha was the first to speak, croaking, "You talked...to a human? No wonder Ankou pulled you back, dude."

"I hope you've got a good reason, mate," Gabe intoned, his face grim as he gave a polite nod at Elizabeth. "No offence, er...Elizabeth."

"I have," Ryder snapped in protest, tightening his hold. "I care about her. And Thomas. And I don't give a shit if that's against the rules, but right now I don't have time for a run down or a lecture. We've got to get moving."

"How can you even see us?" Alisha whispered, striding over to Elizabeth and squinting her eyes at her, as though deciding whether or not the human before her was actually real. Waving her hand back and forth, she added, "You can see us, right?"

"Yes. Shouldn't I be able to?" Elizabeth frowned, glancing over to Ryder for explanation. He gave a sigh, rubbing at his temples. "And who's this 'Ankou'?"

"Ankou is one of the Guardians of the Dead. And no, you shouldn't even have been able to see me, but you could. I thought it was strange, but I didn't question it at the time. I was too caught up in everything, I didn't care." Peering up at the others and fixing them with a cold, hard stare, he remembered the Warders in the bar. "There's something else. I found out the Warders were going to take Thomas before they actually did —that's how I nearly got there in time, before Ankou pulled me back. They were talking about how Empusa wanted Thomas for herself."

Gabe strode across in two great strides, encompassing the flat as though he were a giant in a dollhouse, grabbing Ryder by the shoulder so firmly that Ryder nearly hissed from the strain on his bones. "Are you sure about this?"

"Yes."

"Shit. We've got to move, now. Elizabeth, you're coming with us."

Ryder glanced from Gabe to Elizabeth in concern, his stomach twisting at the fearful urgency in his friend's voice. "What's wrong?"

"She—and Thomas—might be Searchers."

"Searchers?" Ryder's mouth dried up at the word, his gut squirming at the word as though he already knew it was something that only increased the danger Thomas was in.

"Searchers. Humans who are able to seek out souls who are about to die. Sometimes they get mixed up for clairvoyants." Tilting his chin back at Elizabeth, Gabe asked sharply, "You ever felt that?"

Letting out a heavy breath, Elizabeth gave a careless shrug. "Yes," she admitted quietly. "Several times before, and...and...when Thomas died tonight." She glanced down at the floor, her long sheet of hair falling across her face and obscuring it from view, but Ryder could see the lump going through her throat as she swallowed it back. "It woke me up. I've always thought it was gut instinct. Or a sixth sense."

There was a soft whispering of fabric as Mika squeezed through her companions to the young woman, wrapping her arms around Elizabeth. Mika smiled up at Ryder, making soothing sounds as she patted the younger woman's back. He raised an eyebrow at the display of affection, he had never had Mika down as the comforting one. *Guess I'm still learning about the others.*

Mika pulled away, her eyes haunted. "It basically is. Empusa would give anything to have more Searchers—it might mean she would have an edge on us finding people before she did."

Blood drained out of Ryder's body as the gravity of the situation slammed into him, almost winding him as he took stock of the situation. His heart hammered against his ribs as he rose his gaze to Gabe, who was staring back with horror in his eyes. Taking charge, Ryder tapped Mika on the arm, gesturing back towards Thomas' room with his thumb. "Mika, you need to stay here."

"But—"

"You need to watch over Thomas while we're gone. Please. For Elizabeth."

The dark-haired beauty snapped her mouth shut as she took in Elizabeth's sniffling form, giving a tense nod. "Okay, I'll stay," she replied quietly, squeezing Elizabeth's arm in a comforting manner. "But where are you guys going? I don't know where Helheim is."

Now for the portal to Helheim. Where the fuck would it be? Greek said the object from Thomas would help. Chewing it over in his mind, Ryder closed his eyes and tried to concentrate on the background feeling, the one that was so often pushed aside in favour of logic. But logic went out of the window when you were striding around with an energy gun and chasing demonic beings that disappeared in a lick of fire. He gently took hold of the blanket from Elizabeth's outstretched hand, returning her hopeful gaze as he rubbed the soft fibres. It was lemon-coloured, worn through constant use. He held it close to his chest, concentrating on the smell, the texture as his mind flittered through images. Thomas as a baby, cradled in Elizabeth's arms. Thomas using the blanket as a cape, pretending to fly. The blanket draped over the knees of Thomas and Elizabeth as they watched TV together. Then the blanket being left behind as he was carted off to hospital that dreadful night. Ryder squeezed his eyes tighter as the memory of the boy's scream ripped through his skull, the Warders chuckling as they closed in on him.

As he thought back to the Warders from the bar, he gave a low gasp, the realisation hitting him. The blanket seemed to warm to his grasp, and the tattoo on his arm gave a hiss as it burnt against his skin. Elizabeth gave it a wary glance but said nothing, seeming to be overwhelmed enough without asking about more strange goings-on. "I know where it is. We need to go back to the bar, where I saw them. It's somewhere near there, I can feel it."

McKenna moved first to the door, tilting her head back with determination written in her normally soft brown eyes. "Then we need to move, now. If Empusa gets Thomas before we do...I don't want to think of the consequences."

It was here. He could really feel it. The nightclub was silent now, smashed bottles rolling against each other with sticky globs of oddly-coloured alcopops on the pavement just outside, the scent of sex and vomit blending together and filling the air with a sickly sweet tang. But the alleyway down the side gave off a strong vibe straight away as he pulled up on the bike. A whiff of sulphur hit his nostrils, and his pupils widened at the smell. Waving the others forwards, Ryder reached behind to feel for Elizabeth's hand, pulling her forwards and keeping her by his side. Gabe had followed in his car, a bright red modern Mustang that held the others, gleaming menacingly in the glow from the streetlights. Its engine died down with a final growl, and four car doors slammed together as the rest of the reapers piled out.

The group of seven filtered through into the narrow side of the building, picking their way past the stench of the wide metal wheelie bins, steam rising from a nearby drain in the cold air as someone ran hot water through it. There was a large chain-link fence at the far end, blocking off any further entry. Ryder stomped forwards, his boot disappearing into a pile of mulch and debris as he studied the space.

"Well, it looks like this was the wrong place," Gabe muttered in a disappointed tone. "I don't know what we meant to find, really. A swirling vortex of flames, sitting in the middle of the city?"

"Sh," Ryder whispered, narrowing his eyes at the distance between himself and the chain-link barrier. He could feel Elizabeth's clutched hands on his arm, tightening as he focussed on the glimmer of air his sharp eyes had caught. The air shimmered again, glinting as though it were made of fine spider webs. Ryder put his hand out, and gave a harsh intake of breath as the skin burned with sudden heat. "It's here. They're hidden it somehow, but it's here. I can feel it."

Shoving both Ryder and Elizabeth aside, Alisha drew near with a grin, pointing her gun straight for the spot. "Stand back, amateurs," she crooned. "*This* is how you find a portal." Squeezing her trigger finger, she let a blast of white energy explode towards the fence and the glimmering air, Elizabeth letting out a shocked cry as the energy blinded the group for a moment. As they twisted back to stare at the damage, the energy spiralled for a few seconds, before fading and revealing an eddying cycle of fire. It twisted around in a whirlpool of flame, howling with an otherworldly moan as it lit the staring faces with a fiery orange glow. Turning to Gabe with a smirk, Alisha twirled her gun in her palm, remarking, "There's your swirling vortex of flames. You're welcome."

"So...what do we do now? Just jump in?" Elizabeth asked with a tremor in her voice, her green eyes shimmering in the heat of the flames like molten emeralds.

"Guess so," Ryder muttered, gingerly putting his hand out to the odd entrance. As he passed his fingers through to the other side, he was pleasantly surprised to find that although the vortex was warm, it didn't set him alight. Elizabeth followed his actions with somewhat more trepidation, swallowing hard as she found that she too was safe from the flames.

One by one, the group surged forwards and strode into the darkness beyond the vortex, completely unaware of what might lay on the other side. As McKenna passed through, bringing up the rear, the wailing pool of fire spun a few times before disappearing behind them with a loud pop. Whatever happened, it was too late to go back now. They were in Helheim.

CHAPTER SIXTEEN

As the vortex closed behind them, the group were confronted with a long tunnel carved from solid rock, greying shapes hewn from the natural slabs of granite. A cold wind drifted through, picking up in speed as it whistled along to the seven strangers, howling as it bounced from the rocks. With a grim face, Ryder clasped Elizabeth's hand and strode forwards, reaching for his gun with the other.

The remainder of the group followed suit, trudging behind as they drew to the end of the tunnel, tension thick in the air as they prepared to see what lay beyond. As the wind died down at the mouth of the shaft, McKenna let out a low gasp, echoing everyone's thoughts. Ryder wasn't sure what he had expected, perhaps the typical idea of a land bathed in fire, demons with pointy sticks. But not this.

The passage gave way to a wide bridge, spanning the width of a rushing torrent of water, a river that skirted the island in the centre. Mist swirled over the cold, grey landscape, drifting silently in white clouds as it disappeared into the dark waters. Desolation was etched into every surface, and it seemed almost as though the place was uninhabited, if it hadn't been for the chilling wails and cries that echoed from the island.

Just as Ryder took his first step onto the bridge, a menacing growl reverberated through the air. He thrust Elizabeth behind him, as Gabe and Alisha stepped to the fore with their weapons raised, features taut with concentration. Through the mist, the large figure of a hound melted into being. It was at least as high as the reapers, coated in black fur that was matted and sticky with blood. It turned its red eyes on the group, and with a reproachful howl, charged for them.

Alisha was the first one to move, dropping to grab a large knife from her half-laced boots, balancing it on the tip of her finger. As she narrowed her eyes, she took aim, and thrust it towards the creature's eye. It gave an angered yelp as the blade buried itself, the eyeball bursting as it was pierced. Alisha gave a triumphant whoop, pumping the air with her fist as she yanked her gun free, sending a blast of energy into the hound's side.

Gabe rounded the beast as it launched for her, squeezing the trigger on his magnum-style gun, sending an explosion of white light into the hound's thigh. The force of the energy was enough to create a gash in its hind leg, but it did nothing to slow it down as it opened its maw towards Alisha.

She cried out as the creature snatched her about her waist, lifting her into the air and shaking her from side to side like a ragdoll. Blood mixed with the saliva pooling from its jaws, and Alisha gave a pained yell as she twisted in its mouth, attempting to fire at it with her gun. Ryder immediately took off at a run as he left Elizabeth's hand, sprinting as he raced at the creature's side, leaping up onto its back as he fired a blast of energy from Greek's gun with a ferocious shout.

The energy barrelled into the back of the hound's head, and it let out a mournful howl as it dropped Alisha to the ground like a sack of potatoes. Elizabeth and McKenna both raced over to her, helping her up from the ground as the creature thrashed about, twisting its head to try and get at Ryder. He clawed his fingers into the thick fur of the beast, clinging on as it bucked and arched to throw him off. Devin and Drew both ran to his aid, dropping to a knee at the same time and aiming their weapons, firing in unison into the hound's front.

The combined effort of the twins had an effect, as the creature keeled forwards with a baleful cry, its front torn open and collapsing as Ryder took his chance. He pulled himself forwards with gritted teeth and reached for the knife Alisha had thrown, still locked in the eye-socket of the beast. He grasped the handle and tugged, but it wouldn't come lose. Before it came free, the hound rolled over onto its back, unable to carry its enormous weight as the wounds set in, taking Ryder with him.

"Ryder!" Elizabeth screamed, pawing at McKenna's arm. "Do something, he'll be crushed!"

Ryder gave a wheeze as the heaviness of the creature came crashing down on top of him, trapping him against its sticking fur and the gritty hardness of the bridge beneath. Shoving against the crushing dead weight, he gave a further tug at the knife, willing it to come away. It slid in his sweat-slicked hand, and black stars danced in front of his eyes as his lungs deflated from the lack of oxygen. Almost missing the knife altogether, he gave a final yank, and it finally sprang free of the bone with a sickening crunch. Gasping as hard as he could, he lifted the glinting blade, bringing it down to the hound's throat. He collapsed backwards as it found its target, letting out a spray of arterial blood. The hound gave a grunting snap of its jaws, before its red eyes become glassy and misted over with the surrender of death.

Gabe, Devin and Drew all rushed at the creature's body, heaving it free of their friend as he kicked and wriggled his legs, using the last of his strength to shove away from the clumps of fur. With a harsh, relived suck of air, he popped from underneath, leaning against the support of the stone wall that ran on either side of the bridge. Elizabeth flew to his side, dropping to her knees as she put her hands out to him, checking for injuries. "Are you okay? You scared me there."

Ryder twisted his head to look at her, still heaving for breath, a smile crossing his lips. Placing a limp hand against her cheek, he rasped, "I'm good. It's a scratch."

"Any more 'scratches', and we're going to have a hard time reaching Empusa," Gabe pointed out, wiping the back of his hand over his perspiring forehead. "I think we need to adopt a more stealthy approach from here on in, no more charging in like we own the place."

As the others murmured their assent, Elizabeth helped Ryder up, gazing up at him with a worried frown. He wrapped his arm around her shoulders, hugging her close as he stepped in behind Gabe, cracking his neck. "Agreed. But somehow, I think Empusa might be expecting us. You don't just kill the front guard and waltz in, then expect a warm welcome."

They carried on up the road, steam rising from between cracks in the pavement, only the click of their boots making any sound. The fog grew thicker as they came over the bridge and onto the island, reaching an area that looked like a deserted town. Buildings were collapsed on themselves, rubble and debris lying scattered across the roads, windows smashed into gleaming teeth of glass. Wails and moans travelled from the buildings on gusts of wind, howling around the ears of the group. White, ghostly faces travelled through the air and vanished before their eyes, mouths gaping like *The Scream.*

As they rounded a corner, two voices came rasping towards them, somehow more familiar and solid than the pitiful cries of the tormented souls that managed to drift on the edge of Helheim. Ryder found himself pulled back by a strong hand, taking Elizabeth with him. He twisted back sharply, to be met with Alisha placing a finger over her lips and jerking her head towards the direction he had been pulled. The remaining reapers dived into the vacant darkness of the decrepit house, ducking down as two black figures came into view through the fog. Ryder crouched over to a nearby window, peering upwards from the corner so that he couldn't be seen. His eyes widened as he took in the lumbering, deformed shapes of two Warders. They snuffled loudly, sniffing the air as though trying to pick up a scent. Diving back under the window as one of them turned their head, Ryder placed a hand over his thudding heart, whispering, "Warders. Two of them, that I can see. They're looking for us."

"Shit," Alisha muttered, clenching her hand as she brought it down from her mouth. Glancing over at the others, she gave a hard shrug. "We're going to have to take them on."

Just as she reached for her gun, Devin put his palm out towards her, gesturing for her to put it back. "Wait...there might be a better way of doing this than just running out and attacking them."

"Oh, yeah?" she hissed back, an eyebrow delicately raised. "And what do you suggest, Einstein? In case you hadn't noticed, we're on *their* turf."

"Exactly. Their environment, their rules. Let's use it against them."

"How?"

"Well, they're sniffing us out right now."

"So?" Ryder scoffed incredulously.

"So," Devin patiently explained with a huff, "it's important. They catch our scent, we're done for. But not if we're not actually here. And our 'scent' is made up of any number of chemical scents from washing and perfumes." Devin reached inside the sleeveless, ripped denim jacket he wore, pulling out a small bottle of aftershave.

Drew raised an eyebrow at his twin, hiding a smile. "Really? Aftershave on a dangerous rescue mission?"

"Hey, don't judge me," Devin protested, waving the square glass bottle in one hand. "There might be hot women down here." Ignoring the rolled eyes from the rest of the group, he popped the cap off, squeezing the atomiser and spraying large quantities of cheap, musky fragrance around the dilapidated room. He emptied half the bottle before placing it back into his jacket pocket, jabbing a thumb towards the rear of the building. "Now let's get out of here. That should keep them confused long enough for us to get out of sight."

Moving quickly, the seven of them edged their way to the back of the collapsed building, stepping silently over rubble and bricks, a steady drip of water splashing onto them from the ceiling as they passed through to the fog at the rear of the street. The Warders still hadn't got close, but they could be heard sniffing and whispering to one another, echoing through the shell of the house.

"*Go,*" Gabe mouthed silently, ushering the others ahead of him. They weaved down alleyways, holding back coughing fits every time the mist thickened like pea soup, remaining crouched until they reached the end of the long, dilapidated row of houses. McKenna, at the head of the group, craned her neck to peer around the corner of the last building, her dark eyes darting back and forth. The Warders were nowhere in sight, suggesting that Devin's trick had worked, and they would be kept busy searching the entrance for some time.

"They're gone. Now what?" she hissed, her sleek afro bobbing in the breeze that swirled around their heads. She pressed her hands against the wall to steady herself, twisting back to stare questioningly at the others.

"Now we need to make our way...up there," Ryder replied hoarsely, turning his chin to gaze up to his left. The deserted, howling street gave way to a thick, black forest, winding its way up a steep hill. The hill rose in height until it resembled a small mountain, ending in a tall castle with twisted black spires and towers, a wailing mass of fiery clouds hovering around its top. The forest was dark, black as pitch, and strange cries and moans could be heard echoing out from it, the trees twisted and bent with a canopy of dark green leaves. Ryder swallowed nervously, his stomach twitching at the thought of trekking through it with Elizabeth. Almost unconsciously, he wrapped an arm around her waist, hugging her closer. She gave a smile, her slim fingers landing on his arm and squeezing through his jacket. His heart leapt at the touch, the warmth of her palm felt even through his layers of clothing.

Making sure to keep low, the group made their way into the outer reaches of the forest, their feet crunching on the carpet of fallen twigs and dry grass. The trunks grew in number as they ventured further in, and the group straightened themselves up behind the deep cover of the forest. Gabe gave a low sigh, rubbing hard at his lower back. "Thank fuck for that," he muttered. "I was starting to think I'd be that height forever."

A path wound through the centre of the trees, snaking its way up the hill, disappearing into the tapestry of leaves and darkness. Gabe took the lead alongside McKenna, both of them moving forwards carefully and keeping their energy guns at the ready. Ryder and

Elizabeth came after them, followed by Alisha, with Devin and Drew bringing up the rear. No one spoke for several minutes as they went deeper into the forest, all of them listening with thudding hearts to the malevolent cries and screeching wails around them.

As they came to the edges of a large clearing, lit up by an apparently absent moon, Gabe and McKenna both cucked down at the same time. The others followed suit, falling in line as they moved around to see whatever had startled them so much.

Highlighted by the moonlight, its great back rising and falling with snarling breaths, was a huge creature at least ten-feet in height. Its skin was completely black, as though it had been burnt into charcoal, and four wide, leathery wings stretched out from its back, cracked and lined with thin veins. A wickedly-sharp spear rested in its oversized hand, although it looked primitively made.

"What the hell is that?" Elizabeth whispered in awe, her eyes growing as wide as saucers at the sight.

"It's a Megir," Alisha groaned, palming both her gun and the blade by her ankle in one continuous movement, taking in a heavy breath. "They're the infantry of Empusa's little empire—but still a bitch to kill. They're lumbering bastards, and you can always run faster than them, but they're nifty with those spears of theirs. And...they spit poison too."

Ryder raised an eyebrow as he glanced over his shoulder. "How do you know all this?"

Alisha gave a self-indulgent smirk. "You know those things called 'books' we have back at the pool club? You should pick one up sometime."

He tutted at her statement, but couldn't help his lips curling into a grin at her humour. "Alright, so how are we going to do this? I assume we're going to have to get the spear out of his hand."

"No luck there, mate," Gabe broke in, his wrist cracking as he adjusted the hold on his gleaming weapon. "The spear is attached to their hands. We need to just take it down, and fast. The spear is one problem, but I'm more worried about the poison. You get that on you, you're not getting out of Dodge." He shook his head grimly. "There could even be more of them nearby, but we'll have to risk attacking. There's no way we can sneak by it. If we get seen, we don't have the upper hand."

"And we do now?" Elizabeth queried, her features drawn and tight, colour drained from her cheeks.

"Well, we've not been seen yet. If two of us sneak up behind it while two of us go and distract it from the other side, we might have a chance. It's strong enough that a single blast of energy won't kill it, but combined they might. Especially with Ryder's new supergun." Gabe informed them, nodding over to the sleek weapon in Ryder's hand.

Ryder gave a wry smile, twirling a finger across the barrel. "You can thank Greek for this." Turning to Elizabeth, he gazed over at Devin and Drew, both regarding the others silently as they summed up the situation. "Elizabeth, you need to stay with Devin and Drew. Stay out of sight until it's clear."

"No, I'm not sitting here while you all risk your lives!" she hissed, clawing her hand as she clung to Ryder's arm.

He glanced up towards Gabe, who gave a stern, nearly imperceptible shake of his head. Sighing, Ryder repeated the motion at the woman glaring back at him, firmly removing her arm and jerking his head for Devin to come across. "I mean it, Elizabeth. We can't be killed that easily." He fixed her with his icy-blue eyes, the turmoil he felt rciling in his chest clear as he added in a low tone, "I don't want to have to come back here for *you* too. Okay? Stay with them."

For a moment, she looked as though she would protest again, her mouth open on a silent word. Snapping her lips closed again, Elizabeth gave a sharp nod, releasing her hold on Ryder's arm. "Okay," she replied in a cracked voice. "But you better come back."

Ryder grabbed her hand in a snatched movement, pulling it to his lips and kissing the delicate knuckles. "I will. I've no plans on being a kebab."

Gabe motioned towards McKenna, and she moved forwards with him, both of them creeping into the edge of the clearing, gliding through the tall grass that surrounded the glade. Alisha caught Ryder's arm as she swept in the other direction, and he was pulled along as they went the other way to creep up on the unsuspecting creature. It continued to snuffle with each laboured breath, almost as though it was sleeping. They darted behind it, raising their weapons and remaining poised as they waited for McKenna and Gabe to make an appearance.

They didn't have to wait long. Leaping out of the undergrowth, the two reapers charged towards the beast, firing their guns at the same time. The two blasts of white went straight for its upper half, making its head rear back as it let out a bellowing roar. Ryder's stomach lurched as he finally caught sight of the creature's face, a mass of gnashing fangs and melted skin, two black eyes lost in the folds of its fat. They moved quickly, darting out of the way as it rose up to swing the spear at them, missing McKenna by a few hairs.

Alisha and Ryder sprang into action, hitting it from the back. Gritting his teeth, Ryder stood upright and took aim, triggering the force of energy at the Megir's pimpled back. It sank through the flesh, leaving a searing burn and a wisp of smoke that trailed off into the air. The Megir whirled around with a snarl, jabbing the spear rapidly at Ryder's head. Pulse racing so hard it made his head ache, Ryder let out a yell of surprise, tumbling backwards as he tried to avoid being stabbed. The creature persisted, bringing the sharpened point down to his chest, its fetid breath covering him. Before it got the chance to drive the weapon through his chest, Ryder brought the shield on his arm up above his head and rolled out of the way, thrusting his gun up and firing it again at its open mouth.

The beast gave a choking howl, the energy entering its mouth and burning its tongue as black as its eyes, a large clawed hand coming up to clutch at it. Alisha ran across and grabbed Ryder's arm, helping him up before it could attack again. McKenna and Gabe were still the other side of it, attacking with everything they could throw at it, pained expressions covering their features as they took aim. The Megir spun around again, this time keeping the spear back as it opened its maw with a screech. Gabe's eyes widened, and he pushed McKenna out of the way as he dived to one side, taking her with him. A hiss of green liquid spewed out from the beast's open jaws, landing where the two reapers had stood only seconds before. It burned into the dry grass as though it was acid, leaving charred patches in its wake.

"What now? It's not working!" Ryder cried out, dodging behind a large rock as the creature twisted around, still spouting venom as though it was a watering can full to the brim. He darted out again, ringing off another blast of energy at the creature's side, but it simply gave another screech and continued spraying the poison in Alisha's direction.

"Keep going!" Gabe yelled back, panting hard from his exertions. "We'll wear it down eventually!"

The Megir twisted around towards the shouted conversation, screeching as it bumbled forwards with sluggish movements, aiming the venom high against the tree trunks, hoping to catch the reapers. Ryder glanced over his shoulder at the beast. His already short breath caught in his throat as he spied something in the beast's mouth, and he pulled himself back behind the tree hurriedly as the stream of violently green liquid spilled out behind him. The trunk hissed in protest as the poison ate through its blackened bark, creaking as though it would fall over.

Ryder twisted the other way to look for Alisha, his eyes roving nervously across the clearing. When the creature had attacked, they had become separated, but he knew she couldn't be far away. To his relief, he saw a flash of red hair and the gleam of her gun barrel, and crouched out to shout across, "Alisha! Go for its mouth! When it opens its mouth, you can see its heart!" He was sure it had been a heart, the reason for his shock as the creature had spun around. Throbbing like a wild thing, it was balanced at the base of the Megir's mouth as it lowered its jaw to attack, pulsing faster than he would have thought possible. Ryder didn't know how he was so sure hitting the heart would bring it down, but the squeeze in his stomach told him to trust his instinct, just as Greek had advised.

For a moment, Alisha's head appeared across the glade as she nodded over at Ryder, gripping her gun with a determined expression. As the Megir turned in her direction, groaning as it shifted its enormous weight, she ran a nervous tongue across her lips, bringing a hand up to tuck an errant strand of red behind her ear. Perching herself like a cat ready to pounce, she leapt up, swinging her hands up with the gun aimed at the beast's jaws. It swung around at the last moment, moving faster than anyone thought it would, spraying its noxious venom straight towards her.

Ryder's cool eyes widened in fear, and he crouched out from behind the tree. "Alisha, *get down!*"

"No! I can get it!" she cried back, gritting her teeth and holding her stance. As the Megir lined up with her, she fired a blast of energy straight into its mouth, the white light hitting the pulsating heart at the back of its throat with skilled accuracy. As she fired the gun, the creature spewed liquid towards her face, and a stream of it landed straight in the direction of her left eye.

Ryder and Gabe leapt out at the same time, McKenna not far behind them, racing towards Alisha. She gave a bloodcurdling scream, falling backwards to the grass as she clutched at her face, rolling in agony. The Megir stumbled backwards as it attempted to stay upright, black blood pooling from the corner of its wide slit of a mouth as the spear waved about wildly, before it fell backwards with a deafening crash. It thudded onto the forest floor, the resulting dead weight shaking the ground as though an earthquake was coming, crows flying up from a nearby cluster of trees and cawing in wild protest.

"Alisha, are you alright?" Gabe asked breathlessly, dropping to his knees beside her, his gun falling to one side as it was momentarily forgotten. Ryder and McKenna stood nervously behind him, watching in horror as he gently placed his hands over Alisha's, trying to pry them away. She screamed as he tried to pull them back, kicking him away as she scrambled backwards.

"No! Don't touch me, it burns!" she begged, keeping her other eye clamped as tightly shut as her hands on the left side of her face, a tear squeezing from the corner and rolling down her dirt-streaked face. Gabe grabbed her shoulders, pinning her in place as she struggled, jerking his head over to McKenna. She came down next to them, making soothing noises as she tried to prise Alisha's hands apart.

"Sh, it's okay, honey. We have to see, otherwise we can't help." Alisha calmed a little at her words, and she gave a sob through her gritted teeth, allowing McKenna to pull her protection away from her eye. Ryder swallowed back a lump of horror as he cast his gaze over the damage. There was nothing left of her eyeball, leaving just a hollow black space where it had once matched the bright grey eye on her right. The flesh around the socket was mangled together, as though it had been pressed against hot coals and melted away, scarred and raw with the exposed tissue beneath.

Alisha darted her remaining good eye over the others, taking in their horrified silence as she whispered hoarsely, "How bad is it?"

"Well…" McKenna started uneasily, wincing as she tried to think of the right words, "it's pretty bad. But you'll live. It looks as though the poison literally stopped where it hit, and there's no bleeding, amazingly. Put it down to you being a reaper."

"I thought we couldn't die?" Ryder croaked, his heart falling into the pit of his stomach at his words. His legs felt weak. *This is bad.*

Gabe gave a heavy sigh. "It's not that simple, mate. We can't die, and normally we can't be injured, either. But things are different here, it's not the mortal plane. We can be injured here."

Alisha gave an exasperated grunt, jabbing a finger towards her eye socket. "Hello? Can we have this chat later? I believe," she gave another sob, which turned into a sardonic laugh, "I've lost an eye."

"Sorry, Alisha," McKenna murmured, helping her friend to her feet, keeping her gaze trained on Alisha's face. "We'll have to patch you up somehow." Twisting her head, she looked over towards the three figures waiting at the far end of the glade, keeping out of sight still. "Guys, you need to come over here!"

The mood was solemn as Devin and Drew emerged, keeping Elizabeth safely between them as they made their way across, their jaws falling open at the sight of Alisha's eye. She waved a hand at them in mock annoyance, attempting a chuckle. "I know. I'll never wear mascara on both eyelids again."

"Oh my goodness...Alisha, I'm so—"

Alisha gave Elizabeth a stern glare. "If you say 'sorry', I'll ignore you for the rest of this trip. Don't mention it, okay?" She let out a harsh breath. "I can't stand pity at the moment, guys. Just help me get it fixed up so we can get on and get the hell out of here." Her voice cracked as she spoke, as though she was holding tears back in the back of her throat.

"Here, this might help," Elizabeth spoke up, bending down for a moment and reaching for the hem of her dress. Before anyone could stop her, she gripped the edge tightly in her fists, and ripped a large ribbon of fabric free. Holding the frayed length of material in her hands, she carefully placed the centre of it over Alisha's missing eye, pulling the two ends behind her head and tying them in a firm knot. Standing back to admire her handiwork, Elizabeth gave a shy nod, smiling as she explained, "There. It's not your style, but it should help keep it clean until you can sort something else out."

Alisha gave a wry grin, lifting a hand and feeling

across the weave of flowery-patterned fabric gingerly. "It's great," she admitted, reaching across and giving Elizabeth a half-hug with one arm awkwardly, stepping back as she added, "Thanks. Really. And forget what I said about ignoring you. You know I wouldn't do that."

"We should get moving again," Gabe broke in, holding his gun up as he pulled back the pin, checking it as though he was worried it might be low on the endless energy it produced. Ryder watched him thoughtfully, deciding it must be a nervous habit his friend had. It seemed all of them had nervous habits of some kind, if only to keep them sane. Glancing around at the others, Gabe continued, "There could be more of them lurking about It won't take them long to pick up the scent of this dead one, and I don't fancy taking on a pack of them."

CHAPTER SEVENTEEN

The forest trek passed more quickly than they thought it would, as they kept to the edge of the trees rather than the main path. A few more Megirs shambled back towards the shade of the clearing long left behind, their rotten breath curling the leaves of the dying trees as they passed, but luckily didn't spot the seven figures hiding in the darkness. As the trees thinned out, the ground below grew harder, cracking in places as though no water had ever found its way into the dry soil.

Ryder looked up towards the menacing castle above, narrowing his eyes as he caught sight of movement within the swirling mass of fire above. Tugging at Gabe's sleeve as he passed, he pointed upwards and muttered, so Elizabeth wouldn't hear, "What is that? I thought I saw a tail." Elizabeth was a few paces back, walking alongside McKenna and Alisha as Devin and Drew continued to fall in behind.

Gabe nodded, and gave a broad, wry grin. "No doubt you did. It's the Drekar, guards of her castle. They're basically dragons, and they live in that overheated ball of flame, so you can imagine they have no problem breathing it. They shouldn't be a problem though, provided we don't trigger off any alarms."

"Oh, that easy, huh?" Ryder replied drolly, rolling his eyes. "I'll bear that in mind. And can't anything have a normal name down here?"

"What, like 'dragon'? That word wasn't normal, once."

Giving a chuckle at his friend, Ryder shook his

head. "You know, I think I liked you better when you were yelling at me, Oh Great Yoda of the Reapers."

Gabe grinned back, and glanced over his shoulder at the others, still trailing behind. Waiting for them to catch up, his smile fell, and he cautioned, "Everyone has to stick close now. There's nowhere to hide until we get to the castle, but there should hopefully be no one to spot us. There's no windows on that thing, that I can see," he jabbed a thumb towards the gigantic building, "and if Empusa can see us through other means, hiding wouldn't do much anyway. I suggest we move fast, and don't stop for anything. Agreed?"

Everyone nodded as one, and turned their faces to search the landscape set out before them. As the trees petered out, the grass and weeds gave way to cracked mud, the particles of it dried to nothing more than dust that lay on the surface. It was like a desert, devoid of any signs of life, sloping up the steep hill towards the castle. The monstrous building was clearer the closer they got, and the group could make out that Gabe was right, no windows anywhere in the face of its black stone wall. The side facing them rose up into the fiery sky above, ending in disjointed towers of the same stone, sharp spires sticking out at odd angles as though to catch unsuspecting cat burglars. A row of iron teeth ran along the top of the wall, preventing any intruders from simply launching themselves over and entering. The only available entry was a large, ominous gateway that appeared to be unguarded.

Ryder put his hand out towards Elizabeth, grasping her tightly as she came forwards. The others drew in closer, preparing themselves for the flight ahead. The group took off as Gabe waved them forwards, bursting out into the overwhelming heat of the desert landscape. Ryder half-dragged Elizabeth with him, pistoning his legs as he raced towards the castle gate. He could hear the slapping of her sandals against the ground as they ran, keeping perfect time with the erratic rhythm of his pulse as it shot around his body.

He glanced over at the others, keeping pace with them as they stared ahead, focussed on their goal. Shifting his eyes back to the castle, he sprinted hard, his lungs burning with the need for oxygen as the distance grew shorter. Elizabeth cried out as she stumbled over something, and he reacted instantly, grabbing hold of her and swinging her up into his arms. The added weight made him grit his teeth, but he held onto her, sweat dripping down his forehead as the searing heat from above took its toll. Elizabeth clung to his neck as she bounced in his arms, and he could feel her arm bracelets pressing into his skin, leaving an imprint from her tight hold.

A sharp cry came from above, and a moment later, a dark shadow cast over the small group as they sprinted. Gabe darted a look upwards, and immediately pulled his head back, covering it with his arms. "Keep your head covered!" he yelled breathlessly, his throat sounding dry and rasping.

"Why?" Ryder cried back in panic, unable to cover his head as he carried Elizabeth along.

"It's the Hrafnar, Empusa's ravens—they'll use their beaks to peck at us!"

"I've got this," Elizabeth shouted into his ear, covering both his head and hers as she raised her arms. She curved them around so that both their scalps were protected, but her arms were left bare to the mercy of the feathered fiends above. Ryder yanked his head away to try and make her lower her arms once more, but she refused to budge. He growled to himself in exasperation, pouncing his feet until they burned with a deep ache.

The first of the flock descended, diving in a swath of oily black, its fellow crows not far behind as they fell on the group, squawking and screeching as they clawed at hair, jabbing viciously with their sharp beaks. Alisha sliced out with her knife, but the birds simply scattered out of her way, rising into the air with furious cries before falling once more. Drew gave a strangled cry as one of the feathered creatures landed on his head, succeeding in pulling out a clump of peroxide hair in its talons. He lashed out angrily as it gave a cry and glided into the air, splaying his fingers out across the rest of his head.

"Not far now—just run straight inside!" Gabe cried out, waving his arms as he tried desperately to rid himself of a flock of crows, all hovering around him and attempting to strike out with their beaks.

"Got you!" came the triumphant cry from Alisha. A crow had gone for her covered eye socket, not realising that there was nothing but a hollow space behind. It was caught in the fabric, screaming loudly to attract the aid of its comrades, flapping its wings as though it could pull itself free. She grabbed the bird, blood pooling in thin lines from her hands as it scraped its claws over her skin. Yanking it out as she sprinted along, she thrust it behind her, pumping her elbows furiously as she distanced itself. The bird, momentarily disorientated by the sudden drop in elevation, dropped itself to the hard ground before taking flight unsteadily, hovering a short distance behind the other crows.

They finally reached the enormous stone archway of the gates, the thud of their hurried footsteps changing to the clatter of heels on cold flagstones. They raced inside without taking a look around, the temperature from outside dropping to freezing, as if the shadows were the source of the cold air. As Devin and Drew sprinted into the relative safety of the castle, the crows stopped giving chase, halting themselves as though they had come into contact with a pane of glass. They gave enraged screeches before lifting into the sky and retreating to wherever they had come from, the group watching the breathlessly as they panted hard.

Ryder finally released Elizabeth from his grip, letting her slide down from his arms as he slumped against a nearby wall, closing his eyes and allowing the icy stone to seep through to his skin. Every breath he took was painful, burning like wildfire inside his lungs, his skin soaked in sweat. "Tell me...we don't...have to do that again," he wheezed, clutching at his side as a stitch squeezed his muscles.

"I bloody well...hope not," Devin gasped in return, collapsing to the floor as he lowered his head, wiping his hair back from where it stuck to his forehead. Locking mocha eyes with the others, he added, "If Empusa didn't know we were coming, she will now. I'd bet money that those crows were her flying monkeys."

"You're probably right," Gabe admitted grimly, his eyes cold and hard. "We might as well get where we going. Sod hiding, I'm sick of it."

After taking a few moments to check that everyone was uninjured, and had at least caught their breath, the seven of them started off on their journey again. Ryder lifted a hand to Elizabeth's jaw, hooking his finger beneath as he raised her green gaze to his. His eyes traced her face, taking in the fear behind her tight lips, the tension held in her jaw. Leaning in, he gently brushed his lips against hers, closing his eyelids at the exquisite touch of her velvety skin. Pulling back, he placed his palms either side of her face, tucking a delinquent strand of corn-coloured hair behind her ear. "Don't worry, Elizabeth. We're going to get Thomas back."

"I know," she whispered, covering his hands with her own as she looked down towards her feet. "It's just...the closer we get, the more I panic we won't get there in time. I'm scared this 'Empusa' will take him away from me."

Empusa twirled in front of her large, ornate mirror, admiring her reflection. The mirror itself was a gothic work of art, fashioned from the darkest woods, and the deepest black diamonds. Vines twisted themselves over screaming victims, trapped forever in an unholy embrace of pain and torment by the sculptor's hand, demonic creatures grinning wildly at them with sparkling gems for eyes.

But it wasn't the twisted beauty of the mirror that brought a smile to her blood-red lips, it was her dress. Empusa stroked her hands down the length of scarlet silk, draped from her waist to the ground, where it pooled behind her in a trail of fabric, topped by an elaborately embroidered corset. She lifted her hands to fluff her long auburn hair, styled into a high bouffant, the rest left to fall across her back and shoulders. Empusa smiled again at her reflection, her cat-green eyes gleaming as she spun back to face the gnarled female Warder behind her.

"You have done well, Mimi," she called across in her crystalline, authoritative voice. "It's a beautiful dress."

"It pales in comparison to your endless beauty, my Queen," the demonic dressmaker wheezed, bending even lower than her crooked form allowed, splaying out her clawed hands to show her reverence.

Empusa raised an eyebrow, sighing heavily as she waved the Warder away. "Yes, yes...enough sycophantic gestures for one day. Have you got the boy ready yet?"

"Not yet," Mimi rasped, raising her pock-marked face to meet her mistresses, beady black eyes averted from Empusa's gaze. "In a few hours, though. They have not returned with him."

"Good. You may leave now —but don't stray far. I want to know the second the boy is ready for the ceremony." The horned Warder nodded and bowed again, before turning swiftly and shuffling herself from the grand hall, her thudding footsteps echoing and bouncing from the high walls. Empusa stared after Mimi for a moment, lowering her eyes to take in the sight of her attendant's claws. *How does she manage to sew such exquisite garments with those knives for hands? Even I couldn't have predicted that.*

Empusa strode across to the throne at the far end, taking her time as she enjoyed the feel of the silky material caressing her limbs. *Even if I can feel less through some of them.* She sighed as she reached out a hand to lift her skirt, glancing down to gaze upon the bronze legs moving one after the other, both gleaming as they reflected back the candlelight from the walls and chandelier. Part of her curse, Empusa had been given bronzed legs in place of her own, a reminder that she was weighted down, chained forever to her realm in Helheim. It was the reason she had so many Warders —they were her eyes, her ears, her hands outside her gilded prison.

The smile dropped from her lips as she recounted the bitter memories of so many millennia ago. Sweeping around in a flurry of scarlet, she plumped herself down into the high-backed ebony throne, leaning her chin elegantly on her hand as she gazed into space. The room was a grand affair, the largest one in the entire castle, covered from ceiling to floor in rich tapestries and paintings that filled the cold stone walls. A long red carpet ran the length of it, ending at her magnificent throne. It matched the mirror at the far end of the room, and the four-poster bed in the centre, carved by the same hand and studded with glinting black gems. Candles dripped wax from the decadent crystal chandeliers that dotted the ceiling, lighting the room in a soft, glowing embrace.

Empusa sank back into the seat, throwing her arms up in exasperation, blowing out a loud sigh of boredom. She hated to be kept waiting — and especially by a boy A human boy. *But what an important boy he is. The strongest Searcher I've felt in years, even more so than his mother. She'll be next.* Empusa was interrupted from her thoughts by a click at the far end, the double doors swinging open to reveal a small, worried-looking man in a suit. It fitted him perfectly, but the crispness of it was offset by his horns and long black tail, dragging on the ground behind him as he strode up towards the throne.

Empusa sat up straighter, clasping her hands together in her lap as she waited impatiently for her attendant to race towards her, tapping a finger against her other hand. Harry was the only Warder she permitted to go about with a near-human appearance, purely because of the many duties he had carried out perfectly over the centuries. It was a blessing she had never bestowed before, and probably never would again. She knew the deeds he had performed for her kept him up at night. The thought made her lips curl.

Harry stopped short of the throne, dropping into a low bow before straightening himself hurriedly and gasping, "My Queen, we have a problem."

"Problem? *Problem?*" Empusa leapt up from her seat, anger fuelling her veins with sparks as her red hair burst into living flame, an embodiment of what she felt inside. Clawing her painted nails into her palms, she fixed him with narrowed green eyes, hissing, "*Problem* is not a word for gods, Harry."

The wretched Warder dropped to one knee, worrying his hands together as he stammered, "M-My Queen, there are intruders. The crows attacked them as they came over, and one of your Megir lie dead in the forest." He ran a hand through his thinning grey hair, daring to lift his dark blue eyes over the rim of his gold-framed spectacles.

Empusa froze, her heart pounding against her ribs as she allowed another plume of flame to rise up from her head, flickering upwards in a reflection of the candle flames above her. *It can't be. They wouldn't be that stupid. Not for a mere boy.* She carefully stepped down from her throne, her mind whirring as she thought of what to do, Harry shuffling backwards out of her way as she passed. Swinging back around to face him, Empusa jabbed a shaking finger at him, quivering with rage. "Leave them to me. I will deal with them here."

If it really was the reapers...they would not leave in one piece.

CHAPTER EIGHTEEN

The inside of the castle was grimmer than the outside, clad in dark stone and darker shadows. There was barely any light from the sparse smattering of candles, but it worked in the group's favour as they moved silently behind pillars and walls. Gabe and Alisha led the seven of them, darting their heads left and right as they slipped past open archways and doors.

"Wait," Alisha hissed, putting her hand out to stop the others behind from approaching. Gabe crept forwards slowly, keeping his head low as he peered over her shoulder to the reason for their sudden halt.

The passages opened out into a strangely idyllic garden, surrounded on all side by cylindrical pillars and a low wall, a walkway running around them. A tinkling marble fountain and leafy green ferns filled the space inbetween, an impromptu paradise within the foreboding castle. The ceiling was left open, a ray of sunlight appearing from a make-believe sky. Ryder frowned at it, tapping Alisha on the shoulder. "How the hell is that possible?" he whispered, pointing at the golden beams.

Leaning back, she replied, "It's not real—it's an illusion. We must be close, Empusa wouldn't bother with this sort of thing for the Warders."

Just as she spoke, there came the hammering of feet slapping against flagstones, echoing back out to the group. Four Warders became visible in the passageway opposite, hoods covering their long horns and mangled features. They ran towards the garden, ill intent clear on their faces as they pounded along. Ryder flicked his weapon out in a slick movement, the others following suit. Even Elizabeth pulled out the gun Ryder had given her back in the apartment, though her hand shook as she gripped the handle tightly.

Drew was the first to break the tension, giving a loud cry as he leapt over the low stone wall, firing his gun towards the first Warder. It missed the creature's head by inches, and the Warder gave a snarl, sprinting towards the reaper. He dodged aside just as a long horn almost tore through his side, the Warder growling as the twisted instrument scraped instead against the wall, dust scattering from the stones. Drew spun around, half-disappearing into a leafy green plant as he cocked the gun at the Warder.

It turned around slowly in its shuffling manner, grinning widely at the barrel pointed at its face, a row of glinting, sharp incisors that lined the wide gap. It came forwards until the barrel was no more than an inch away, and Drew narrowed his eyes in anger at the creature's forwardness, squeezing his finger gently. The usual blinding slice of energy burst from it, carving its way into the Warder's features. The grin fell as its head caved in, falling limp to the floor with the rest of its body.

The group sprang into action, Alisha and Gabe tag-teaming to take on the second Warder. Having seen the fate of its companion, it drew back with a hiss, the long grasses whispering as its fetid, wobbling body withdrew to the darkness of the pillars and walkway. Alisha bent to the knife in her boot, catching the tip neatly in her fingers as she pulled her arm back, sending it arcing through the air to its target. No one expected what happened next. The Warder didn't have time to sidestep the knife coming for its eyes. A withered hand came out from the dark sleeve of its robe, foot-long claws at the end of each nobbled finger, and it waved the hand with an elegant flourish.

The knife went sailing to one side, clattering against the far wall as it bounced onto the flagstones. Alisha's jaw dropped open as she saw the glint of the metal sliding back through the air, and she twisted her head to meet Gabe's equally amazed expression. "Can they do that?" she cried.

"They can now," he replied grimly, launching himself forwards with his weapon in hand. Diving through the walkway at the side, he snatched up the fallen knife and locked gazes with the demonic beast before sprinting over to stab towards it. As expected, the Warder moved aside again, lashing out with its gigantic claws. Gabe ducked down, giving a sideways glance over to the others. Devin was already racing across to help, firing his gun at will towards the creature's head. Drew and McKenna were busy battling with the third Warder at the far side, diving away from its claws as they fired at it. But each time they let off a blast of energy, the Warder simply lifted its hands and deflected the blast, sending white light smashing into the stone pillars. They groaned under the strain, clouds of ground dust scattering into the air.

Ryder swivelled his head from one fight to another, his palms sweating against the grip of his gun as he tried to decide what to do. His cool eyes travelled across to the far end of the garden, to the passageway where the fourth Warder was stood back from the others, not moving at all. *Why isn't it coming to aid the other Warders?* Ryder's jaw tightened as he realised the final Warder was moving its lips slowly, muttering mystical words to itself that he could barely hear over the cries and shouts going on around him. Turning hurriedly to Elizabeth, he urged, "Stay here. If that one," he paused to point over at his target, "moves towards you, fire the gun.

And run to the others."

Before she got a chance to protest, clutching at thin air as she tried to catch his sleeve, Ryder straightened up and flew across the courtyard to the Warder. The creature's beady black eyes opened as it gave a screech of surprise, putting its palms out flat towards Ryder. A wind picked up out of nowhere, so strong that it robbed the breath out of his chest, shoving him back so hard he had to drop down and thrust the shield up in front of his face. Gritting his teeth, Ryder glanced back up over the top, his skin pulled back from the force of the wind as he locked eyes with the Warder. The creature gave an angry cry, furious that its power could not break the ancient metal as it continued throwing it in Ryder's direction. Realising he was going to have to give before the Warder did, Ryder grunted as he eased the shield further down his arm to reach his gun. Although it felt like a weight pushing down on his arm, he clutched his wrist with his other hand, shoving the gun forwards.

The Warder let out a rasping chuckle, clearly believing this gun blast would be no different from the ones its companions were knocking aside like pillows. Ryder gave a growl at the creature's smug face, and rammed his finger down onto the trigger, sending out an explosion of white light. It was stronger than the others, as it had been before, and it made the ground shake as it smacked into the magical wind that had whipped up. The wind vanished as though it had never existed, reeling the Warder backwards.

Ryder gave a vicious grin at the fallen creature, jumping up and racing across, wasting no time in uploading another blast of energy into the Warder's face. It crumpled in a heap to the ground, the voluminous cloak draping over its face as it croaked out a dying breath. His chest heaving from the exertion, Ryder twisted around with shining eyes to face the others, his heart lifting to see that they were beating back the Warders, now that whatever spell the fourth one had weaved was gone. As the rasping cry of the last Warder drifted through the air, he nodded solemnly, gazing over at the long passageway behind that led to the centre of the castle. To Empusa. "Not long now."

Ryder threw the doors wide open, charging in, a man on a mission. Elizabeth was just behind him, flanked by Gabe and Alisha. The others came up behind them, swinging their weapons left and right, checking for any Warders hiding in the shadows.

At the far end stood a tall, elegant woman in a red dress, her matching hair pulled high on her head. Ryder's eyes widened as he roved his gaze over the miniature inferno, realising the burning red hair was literally in *flames*. She had one hand on her hip, a self-satisfied smile curling her lips as she waited patiently for the group to make their way up towards her. "Good evening, Reapers. What a pleasant surprise," she purred, narrowing her gaze towards Ryder.

He scowled in return, cocking the gun even as his instinct told him it would be useless against her. *Empusa, I assume.* "The pleasure is all yours. Where's Thomas?"

"Tut, tut, Ryder. That's not how we do it," she admonished, mockingly waving a finger. "First we exchange witty remarks, talk about your past...then we come to the little boy."

"How do you know my name?"

"Oh, please." She grinned, revealing straight white teeth as her eyes glowed red. "I know a great deal more than that. My Warders nearly had you that New Year's night. You could have had everything, if you had joined us down here. *I* wouldn't have made you choose between slavery and a life of misery, like Ankou and Morrigan." Empusa spat their names with disgust, her features marring with her revulsion.

Ryder felt Gabe's hand clutching his shoulder tightly, and his friend's deep voice rumbled in his ear, "Don't rise to her bait. She's distracting you."

Ryder shrugged him off with a curt nod, setting his lips in a thin line as he held his stance. His cool eyes flashed with ice as he glared across at the queen, tilting his head back as he replied, "I chose something worthier than I had before. I don't call that slavery. I call that redemption."

"But you could have had all this," Empusa hissed, waving her arms in a figure of eight. Gold coins rained down from nowhere above her head, rattling onto the ground into large piles. Two beautiful young women materialised from behind her, sauntering forwards with come-hither stares, crooking their slim fingers coyly at Ryder. "You can still have it. Riches, women...whatever you want. I'll even let you keep your looks." Empusa grinned wryly, her calm demeanour returning as she added, "All you have to do is let me keep the boy. Help me get rid of your friends, and I'll give you whatever you want."

His eyes flickered from the gold to the two young women, thoughts racing through his head. Someone tugged on his arm, and he twisted to meet the gentle green of Elizabeth's gaze, her face drawn and pale. His heart leapt to see her pain, and he spun back to face

Empusa, drawing his gun up and growling, "Keep your whores and money. I want Thomas, out here, *now*."

Empusa waved her arm once more, and the vision vanished as suddenly as it had appeared. Her lips drew back in a snarl and she took a few intimidating steps forward, close enough that he caught a glimpse of metallic legs beneath her skirts. "Listen, reaper, you're not having him. And may I remind you that you've broken the agreement between the realms? I can do what I like to you now." There was a loud clearing of a throat from behind one of the darkened pillars, and she turned her head sharply before continuing, "But it would seem you have to wait. My ceremony is about to begin."

As the others watched with dread, a wizened old man with horns and a long tail, dressed in an ill-fitting suit, came out from behind the pillar, holding Thomas by the shoulders as he walked him forwards. Elizabeth's cry of happiness rang around the hall as she shouted, "Thomas! Thomas, it's Mummy!"

The little boy turned slowly in the man's hold, and his soft brown eyes popped out at the sight of his mother, his frightened expression holding her rapt in his gaze as he cried, "Mummy! Please save me from the horrible lady!" He struggled to get free, but the demonic man held him tight with a dark chuckle.

Elizabeth ran forwards to him, but Empusa darted one hand out as she cast a bolt of flame in her path. Ryder caught Elizabeth up quickly, wrapping his hand around her waist and pulling her back just as the heated plume of orange missed her. Putting her down again heavily, he angled his head to the others and shouted, "What do we do?"

Gabe, ever the leader, was the first to act. Nodding at the others, he grabbed Alisha's arm and hissed, "Keep Empusa busy, Ryder and Elizabeth will get Thomas!"

Alisha and Gabe both dropped to one knee as they aimed their weapons at Empusa, triggering the flashes of energy into her figure. She returned their fire with ease, sending large balls of flame sailing towards them with a screeching warcry. Drew and Devin fell in behind them, blasting their guns enough to keep her occupied with defending herself as they moved back and forth.

Snatching up Elizabeth's hand, Ryder raced towards the demonic man holding Thomas, who narrowed his eyes and pushed the small boy behind him. Thomas gave a terrified cry as he was shoved, falling backwards hard onto the floor. He let out a gasp, before his tiny face screwed up and he burst into loud wails. Still battling with the other reapers, Empusa gave an angry hiss. "Harry, shut him up!"

The demonic man gave a growl as he nodded over to his mistress, twisting around and scooping Thomas up, giving him a hard shake to prevent him from crying. Ryder's fury reached full peak, and he launched himself at Harry, pointing at Elizabeth and shouting, "Grab Thomas when he drops him!"

"Drop him?" Harry echoed, looking up in shock. Before he had a chance to move, Ryder raised the butt of his gun, bringing it down onto the man's skull. It smashed against his horn, scraping along it as it hit its mark. Harry staggered back, releasing his hold on Thomas enough for the boy to fall to the floor. He snarled, turning on Ryder and lashing his tail towards the unaware Reaper. The spiked end of it caught Ryder on his cheek, leaving a gash of red as he hissed in fury, readying his clawed hands.

"Get off him! He's the good man!" Thomas cried

shrilly, turning around and pummelling his tiny fist into the demonic creature's leg. Harry gave a growl and twisted around to catch hold of Thomas, who neatly darted out of the way and kicked his bare foot into the Warder's shin.

"Shit," Ryder muttered through clenched teeth, falling back and raising a hand to the wound, blood seeping through his fingers and trickling along his skin. Harry grinned maliciously, having taken his eyes off Ryder as he finally grabbed hold of Thomas, who was kicking and punching furiously against his restraint. Using the demonic creature's distraction to his advantage, Ryder sprinted across and aimed his gun at Harry's head. The creature ceased grinning as he took in the gleaming barrel, aligning with Ryder's cold eyes. The trigger squeezed, and a flash of brilliant white light shot out like a bullet, smashing into him with so much force he fell backwards on the floor, choking him as his breath caught. Elizabeth took the moment and snatched Thomas up before he hit the marble ground, holding him tight as she murmured into his ear with tears streaming down her cheeks, stroking his hair soothingly. He buried his face into her shoulder, clinging on with his small arms.

Ryder strode across to Harry sprawled on the floor, the gun pointed at the Warder's forehead. Before Harry even had a chance to whimper, Ryder fixed him with a cool glare, and let out another blast of energy. The white brilliance exploded once again, and when it cleared, Harry's eyes were closed tightly, his mouth ajar from the hit. Ryder's eyes narrowed as he noted the creature's chest rising and falling still with even breaths. *Must have just knocked him out cold. What does it takes to kill these creeps?*

Empusa noticed her fallen sidekick, and let out a terrifying, furious scream, her hair lengthening as the fire grew with her anger. As the others watched with dropped jaws, she jabbed a finger over to Ryder, her eyes blazing with red flames. "Now you're really going to get it. Do you *know* how much I'm going to have to heal that bastard now? I *always* get my way!" She tilted her head back, throwing her arms to the sky, and her form changed before their eyes. She grew in length, her figure widening and growing taller as she rose towards the ceiling, letting out a bloodcurdling cry. Her skirt melted away, revealing her articulated brass legs, looking more like the bottom half of a knight's armour than limbs. As she spread her arms out, two large red winds dropped from them, leathery and jagged. Her hair burst into fresh flame as horns crunched out from her temples, her eyes fading into black vortexes as she glared down at the mass of reapers before her. "Now," she boomed, "my turn."

Her clawed hands curled into fists as she drew them to her chest, crackling energy building up inside them. Elizabeth dragged Thomas into her arms and ran with Ryder to the side of the others. Gabe shook his head solemnly. "This isn't good. Time to run, guys."

They twisted around to sprint for the exit, but the large double doors slammed into place before they got to them. Empusa cackled loudly as they turned to stare up at her with nervous faces, balls of fiery power growing by the second in her furled hands. The goddess raised her arms, preparing to throw the orbs of flame towards her intruders, when a brilliant light burst through the dark ceiling, flooding the hall and surrounding the reapers and their two charges. It was blinding, and most of the reapers threw an arm up over their eyes against it, a familiar chorus of sweet voices whispering and singing around them. Empusa let out a harsh yell, her black eyes widening as she realised what was happening. "No! NO! Morrigan and Ankou, leave them here, you bastards! *They're MINE!*"

Ryder clutched Elizabeth and Thomas tightly to his side, covering Thomas' head to prevent him from seeing any more of the nightmare, stroking the young boy's soft hair as he murmured, "Don't look, Thomas. It's all going to be okay now." His heart thudded against his chest, and he glanced over to the furious goddess with brass legs, hoping he was right. The voices and chanting grew louder around them as the light glowed brighter, and his nerves tightened as he saw Empusa aiming her hands towards them. Empusa's shriek of rage reached fever-point, and she finally let the magic burst towards the group, two glowing, crackling orbs of fire far bigger than all of them. Just before they hit, Ryder felt the familiar lurch in the centre of his belly, and rushing wind pushed at his ears as the group were lifted from their impending death.

CHAPTER NINETEEN

He hit the ground hard, but thankfully stayed on his feet this time, keeping tight hold of Elizabeth and Thomas to prevent them from falling over too. When his vision cleared, Ryder blinked a couple of times, looking around himself in relief as he was met with the marble walls and safety of the Hall of Rest. The others were with him, and there were collective groans and grunts as everyone picked themselves up from the ground, dusting themselves off and checking for any injuries. Remembering the gash to his cheek as it stung him, Ryder felt for the wound with a wince, dabbing it to test how far it spread.

There was a howl of wind, and two tall, familiar figures appeared at the far end. The reapers fell silent as Ankou and Morrigan came forwards, Ankou's hood pulled low over his face, Morrigan's features cold and hard. Ryder's eyes flickered nervously between them as he felt his pulse picking up, hammering against his skin as he awaited the lecture he knew was coming. Ankou was the first to make a sound, stopping just short of the group and hammering his staff against the ground. It clanked, the noise bouncing off the walls like a warning shot as he steadily rose one finger, pointing it sharply at Ryder. "Come forward," he intoned.

Gulping back his anxiety, Ryder passed Thomas over to Elizabeth, even as she grabbed at his shoulder in worry with tight features, proudly coming away from the group and stopping in front of the hooded god. A loud, heavy sigh escaped from beneath the dark folds of the hood, and the silence that followed was laden with tension. A sweat broke out over Ryder's skin, and he placed his hands behind his back, twisting them together in worry.

Ankou lifted his hand and slowly pulled his hood back, revealing his pale head and searching eyes as he passed them over the reaper before him in a disapproving sweep. "Ryder," he began solemnly, his voice booming around the space. "What you just did was the most stupid, the most irresponsible, the *most foolish thing* any of my reapers have ever done."

Ryder hung his head at the guardian's words, nodding silently. He knew Ankou was right. He had put all the others in danger, as well as himself, all because he hadn't carried out his duty in the first place. And little Thomas could have been lost forever, and now the contract between the realms had been broken, all because of his actions. Twisting his fingers together harder, he croaked, "I know. I'm sorry, Ankou."

The guardian sighed again, jutting his chin. "And…we couldn't be prouder of you."

Ryder blinked rapidly, wondering if the rush of nearly being killed, and then being told off like a scolded child had done something to his mind. Raising his head slowly, he fixed wide blue eyes with Ankou, who gave a rare and gentle smile back at him. "Did…did you say…proud?"

Morrigan stepped forwards to stand beside her husband, her features softening as she spoke. "Yes, Ryder, proud. You have changed so much from the selfish, angry young man you were only a few weeks ago. It is true that the contract is now broken between the Hall of Rest and Helheim, but we shall have to deal with that." She paused to glance at Ankou, who returned her sideways look. "One day we were going to have to face it, anyway. You just speeded things up. But you also risked your life to get this young boy back from Empusa, without concern for yourself."

"But it was my fault he was there in the first place," Ryder protested bitterly, aware of the sensation of the eyes of the others on his back. It pricked under his jacket, and he shifted uncomfortably as though he could rid himself of the sensation.

"Perhaps," Ankou broke in. "But you set it right. You would never have done that before becoming a reaper. Your answer to a problem was to run away from it. You have saved Thomas and his mother, and you have proved yourself amongst my most capable of warriors."

A throat cleared from across the Hall, and everyone turned as one to see who it was. Greek was there, leaning against one of the pillars with a broad smirk gracing his lips. Ryder relaxed at the sight of his friend's confidence, and he grinned back. "Well, I didn't do it alone. If Greek hadn't helped me, I would never have been able to—"

"Greek? You helped him to disobey us?" Ankou interrupted, twisting to face his faithful Reaper.

Greek raised his eyebrows and pushed off from the column, sighing and throwing his hands up in the air dramatically. "Oh, please. You and Morrigan have been putting off the inevitable for centuries. I just pushed things along a bit. Empusa would have cracked eventually, and then we wouldn't have had the upper hand. So, yes. I helped young Ryder." He smiled proudly at his protégée. "I knew what he felt. Let's just say it helped me work out some of my personal demons too."

Elizabeth cleared her throat, shifting Thomas onto her hip, and roved her gaze around at everyone. "Is *anyone* going to tell me where we are?"

There was hesitation in the air for a moment, and Morrigan stepped forwards, her red lips curving into a kind smile as she held a hand out warmly. "Elizabeth, we are so sorry. We should have explained. This," she motioned around the room, "is the Hall of Rest. The antithesis of Helheim. It is where souls are looked after and conducted into their next lives."

"Next lives?" Elizabeth repeated nervously, tightening her hold on Thomas, who whimpered at the hold and wrapped his arms about her neck. She glanced over to Ryder, who was watching her with a mixture of pity and self-hatred. He looked away, his chest twisting again. "This...this is where Thomas had to come. Right?"

Morrigan's smile fell, and her blood-red eyes flickered to the tight grip of Elizabeth's hands, before answering in a murmur, "Yes, my dear. And..." She trailed off, taking a deep breath. "And I'm afraid he must still come with us."

"No! I'm not leaving! Tell them, Mummy!" Thomas shouted at Morrigan's words, trembling as his tiny hands clutched in a death grip at Elizabeth's collar, fiercely flashing his eyes at the goddess.

"I'm sorry, Thomas. But your Mummy must let you come with us," Ankou intoned, his voice surprisingly lighter than normal, as though he had purposely done it for the young boy's benefit. "We're not like that nasty lady you met earlier, I promise. We can take you somewhere wonderful, and—"

"No! I'm not going, I'm staying here, with Mummy," Thomas whispered, his bottom lip wobbling as his large green eyes filled with tears.

Ryder took in the sight of the quivering child, clinging to his mother as though he would never let go,

Elizabeth's eyes bloodshot with the tears she was holding in. His stomach lurched. *I can't let them do this. I can't.* Flashes of the next life he had to lead sailed into his mind, and his heartbeat rushed against his temples at the horrendous memory. But it had to be done. Stepping forwards, he announced loudly, "Take me instead."

Ankou blinked for a few seconds, shaking his head in response. "I'm sorry, Ryder. We cannot take you for the next life belonging to Thomas."

"I know that," Ryder bit out, lifting his ice-eyes to stare directly at the guardian. "I mean *my* next life. Please leave Thomas with his mother. It's not fair, not after what they've been through." He gestured at Elizabeth with a shrug, who was gazing back at him open-mouthed. "Let them carry on living, together. They're all each other has. I don't have anyone." He jutted his chin, rolling his shoulders back with a click. He was prepared for whatever came now. He knew it. "I'll take my next life instead. I don't care how shit it is. But let Thomas live."

The other reapers gasped. Even Greek's eyes widened as the cheeky grin fell from his face. Everyone understood what he was asking for. Even if they had never seen the vision of his next life, they had similar tales themselves, or they wouldn't have chosen to be reapers. He wasn't choosing life for a life. He was choosing hell for a life. Elizabeth ran over to him awkwardly with Thomas still balanced on her hip, laying her hand on his arm desperately. Ryder slowly turned his head to look down at her, beautiful green eyes melting into tears as she stuttered, "I-I don't k-know what you're asking for, but you can't! I want Thomas alive, a-and I-I want you alive too! Please don't leave us." Her voice dropped to a whisper. "I need you."

Those three words snatched at his heart and

drew it clean out of his chest, making his eyeballs prickle at the thought of never seeing her or Thomas again. Ryder shook his head, grasping her face gently in his hands. "I have to, Elizabeth. Someone must go. I need you too, but I have to go now. I should have gone before, but I stayed, and I was able to rescue you both. I'm grateful for that." He lowered his face, pressing his lips against hers, savouring their softness, their taste so unique to lovely Elizabeth. She burst into tears against the kiss, but he held her still, forcing the memory so hard into his mind that he would never forget it, even in his next life. Breaking away from the kiss, he smiled weakly at Thomas, who was watching the exchange with surprise in his face, and ruffled the boy's hair. Keeping his hand cupped to the boy's cheek, he croaked, "You look after your Mum, okay? You're both going to be alright."

"No," Morrigan interrupted, her voice firm. Ryder spun around to glare at her with steel in his eyes, their stubbornness grating at him with fury. She held up her hand for silence, stopping him before he could retort as she closed her eyes for a moment, looking as though she were collecting her thoughts. "What I mean to say is, no to you taking your next life, and no to Thomas coming with us too."

Ankou barrelled his staff sharply into the ground, his grey features wrinkling further with anger as he stared daggers at his wife. "Morrigan? I don't believe it is merely your decision."

Morrigan spun on her heel, the crows on her shoulders cawing sharply at the suddenness of her movements. She hissed back at Ankou, tossing her long black hair over her shoulder and disrupting one of the birds, who took off in a flurry of oily black feathers. "Are you really so stubborn, old man? We have the power over life and death, and we are able to make exceptions."

"And the boy makes a speech, and that is the exception? I agree he has shown considerable courage and bravery in coming forwards, and I admire his selflessness, but that is no reason —"

"It is *every* reason. We will need reapers more than ever now that Empusa has free reign. I don't think it's a good idea to lose one." She twisted her head to narrow her eyes at Ryder, one side of her mouth curling into a smirk. "And I think the boy is determined enough to prevent you taking Thomas, that he would fight us. He might even win. But I don't want that, do you?"

Ankou was silent for a moment, glancing between his wife and Ryder, before nodding and lowering his head. "You are right, of course. As usual," he added wryly, earning himself a raised eyebrow in return. He pointed a long, bony finger at Thomas. "And, the young boy and his mother are special. Searchers. Powerful, too. They could help us, I suppose."

Gliding across the floor, his robe rustling on the ground behind him, Ankou approached with intent gleaming in his pale eyes. He placed one hand on Ryder's, patting it in a fatherly manner. Ryder nearly jumped at the icy touch, not expecting it to be as frosty as it was. Gulping visibly, he waited to see what the robed god would say. Ankou paused for a moment, giving one last look over to Elizabeth. "Ryder...you will remain a reaper. And," he continued, holding a finger up and putting his head back as Ryder's mouth opened to speak, snapping it shut again at the gesture. "And Thomas will not be taken today. But it's not safe for them alone anymore. They must remain under your care, do you understand? They are precious, more precious than you or they realise. Searchers are the key to life and death, and they can do more than simply judge when another soul is about to die. Look after them."

Ryder's chest swelled at the god's words, and his chin trembled as he fought his emotions, nodding sharply at Ankou's words. A warm smile broke the guardian's wrinkled face, and the pale eyes lit up for a second with fatherly care before he turned his attention to Thomas and Elizabeth. She released the small boy from her grip and let him sink to the floor, where he stood half-buried in her skirt as he regarded the hooded Ankou with trepidation.

Ankou gave a grunt as he crouched down to look into Thomas' little face, taking in the child's wide green eyes and fist, clutching Elizabeth's in a death grip. Reaching out one hand, he pressed it firmly against Thomas' chest, gazing at him kindly. "Don't worry, little Thomas. You will stay with your mother. But I can't let you go back yet, not while you're poorly. We must make you well again." As the others watched in rapt silence, Ankou kept his hand where it was, closing his eyes and muttering under his breath. The wrinkles deepened as he concentrated, and finally he brought his hand away with a loud popping sound, bringing with it a mass of black and twisted tumour.

Thomas' jaw dropped, and he reached out timidly, giving the black gunk a prod with a tiny finger. His voice an awed whisper, he looked up at Ankou and asked, "Was that in me?"

Ankou smiled again and waved the hand quickly, the tumour disappearing as he revealed his bare palm. "Not anymore. But you and your mother must stay with this man now," he added, pointing over to Ryder. "He will protect you both and keep you safe." Rising back up, he nodded at Ryder, who grinned gratefully back.

"Well, no point keeping them all sat here on their arses," Greek broke in, easing the tension as he jabbed a thumb at the other reapers, who had watched the scene play out before them with bated breath. "Might as well send the gits back." He winked playfully at them, and wrought a smile from Drew and Devin.

Gabe cleared his throat noisily, nodding vigorously. "Yeah, er…we should get back. If that's okay." His eyes were bloodshot, his jaw tense as though he was holding something back.

Alisha gave a snort, her own eyes red with sympathy as she gave Gabe a shove. "Aw, Gabe. I never knew you cared. Not getting soft on us, are you?"

"Hardly," he retorted sharply, giving a casual shrug. His hand came down heavily on Ryder's shoulder, and he gave an uncustomary smile. "Go on. Give her a smacker on the lips and all that romantic shit. You did good, mate."

Ryder gave a chuckle, his shoulders relaxing at the friendly banter, slapping his brother-at-arms in return as he remarked, "Cheers, mate. I might just do that." Twisting back, he paced across to Thomas and Elizabeth. He threw his arms around both of them, breathing in Elizabeth's scent with relish. *I will protect them to the death. This is what I was meant for. This is my purpose.*

CHAPTER TWENTY

"Home, sweet home," Devin chirped merrily, dramatically giving a stretch as he entered the living area, throwing himself down onto a nearby chair. "I could sleep for a month."

"Don't get too comfy, Billy Idol," McKenna spoke up, giving him a friendly hit on the arm as she swept by. "We've got work to do."

The others filtered in one by one, Mika bringing up the rear. She had known the second they were taken, Greek had apparently sent her a message to let her know they were safe and that she had to return home. Such as 'home' was. Elizabeth entered gingerly, picking her feet over the discarded rubbish and clothes as she made her way inside, glancing up at the walls with trepidation. Ryder followed close behind, carrying Thomas over his shoulder. With all the excitement, the small boy had fallen asleep, his thumb stuck in his mouth as he slept. She raised her eyebrows at the boarded up windows, glancing over at McKenna, who was busily trying to scoop up some of the mess with an embarrassed face. "So, er...this is where you guys live? All the time?"

Ryder gave a shrug. "Don't blame me. It was like this when I got here."

Gabe shoved past them carefully, squeezing Elizabeth's arm in a friendly manner as he brushed past, jerking his head towards the mess. "Well...I guess we could do with tidying the place up. We just never got around to fixing it up. I mean, there are other bedrooms, for example, and—"

"There's other bedrooms?" Devin burst out, as his twin sniggered at his brother's response with a shake of his head. "All this time I couldn't bring women back because we've got some kind of Tom Brown's Schooldays set up, and I could have had my own room? I thought they were just full of boxes, or cursed, or something."

Gabe gave him a hard glare, folding his arms across his massive chest and raising his eyebrows. "First of all, you shouldn't be 'bringing women back'. This isn't a bachelor's pad. And secondly, I was thinking more for Elizabeth and Thomas' benefit. Our room isn't fit for a little boy, they need their own space." He paused at Devin's disappointed face, letting out a harsh laugh as he relented, "Fine. You can have your own room, I'm not your keeper. Just keep the noise down, you understand?" Shaking his head at the others, he threw his hands up in mock despair. "Why do I feel like I'm the father?"

"Because you're the tallest," Alisha quipped, shrugging her leather waistcoat off and tossing it down onto the pool table at the far end. She winked at Ryder, who was smiling like a lovelorn puppy at Elizabeth, and smirked. "Besides, you're right. They *do* need their own room. It might be catching." She dissolved into merry laughter as Elizabeth's cheeks flushed red.

Ryder tapped Elizabeth on the shoulder, ignoring the obvious comment as he jerked his head towards the stairs. "Come on, I'll show you the rooms. We'll leave Thomas down here until we've got his room tidied up, I don't want him waking up and thinking he's back with Empusa." He raised his crystalline eyes to McKenna, patting Thomas gently on the back. "Can you watch him for a few minutes?"

She skirted the table in the centre, smiling kindly as she reached up to pull the sleeping child from Ryder's shoulder, easing him into her arms to take him over to the sofa. "Of course," she responded warmly, her smile growing broader as she looking down at the small boy, her face lighting up. "He's an adorable little thing. Take your time."

"Hey!" Alisha cried out, darting across the room to ruffle her hand in Thomas' hair gently. "I can watch him too. He's a rugged little tyke. He needs his Auntie Alisha to teach him how to turn that into fighting spirit."

"What about me?" Mika spoke up indignantly. "I was going to look after him if he came back to the flat, anyway. I can't have you two cooing over him like lost doves He's going to need someone to show him around, and you two don't even know where the fridge is."

Gabe laughed loudly, causing the three women to glance up at him sharply, their eyebrows puckered into frowns. "Look at you three mother hens. Be careful with the boy, there's only one of him to be smothered."

Elizabeth chuckled as she beamed over at the three female reapers, laying her hand on McKenna's arm as she spoke. "I'm glad he's got three aunties now. And uncles, too. I'll never be able to repay what you guys did for us. Never."

In an unabashed display of emotion, Drew crossed the room and caught Elizabeth up in a bear hug, letting her go with a gentle smile. "Don't mention it. You're one of us now. Thomas too." He glanced slyly over to Ryder, who was watching his friend with obvious jealousy, his jaw tense even though he was smiling. "Now I think I better let you go before Ryder pops me one." To Ryder, he winked, and added, "Don't worry, I'm not going to steal her away. Get upstairs and leave us alone, you lovesick git."

Ryder's face broke into a wide grin, and he

shook his head at Drew's comment, retorting, "Thanks, mate. Wait until it happens to you." Still beaming, he took Elizabeth's hand and led her towards the stairs, his heart thumping against his chest with excitement. Her scent surrounded him as they took the stairs, and he closed his eyes once they reached the top landing, letting the fragrance of strawberries and coconut fill every inch of his soul.

Not saying a word, he led her across the upstairs hallway, pushing doors open and peering inside. Finally reaching one at the end, he nodded towards the doorway. "This one seems the cleanest. And it's got a huge bed, and a smaller one too. It's perfect for you and Thomas."

"Fantastic. I'm still going to bleach this place to hell though," Elizabeth chuckled, swinging her blonde hair over one shoulder. Her blush from earlier still hadn't vanished, and Ryder's eyes followed the rosy trail as it spread across her cheeks and neck, dipping over her shoulders into the folds of her top.

"It'll do for now," he rasped hoarsely, stepping backwards and pulling her with him. She let out a delighted cry as she was pulled into the dim light of the bedroom, nearly tripping as he caught her and shoved the door closed in one movement. Ryder smoothed his hand over her hair, pushing her gently back against the wall until she let out a gasp. His glacial eyes took in her figure with appreciation, resting on every curve and hint of skin. *She's the most beautiful creature I've ever seen.* Her green eyes shone with desire as she looked back up at him, her pink lips parted on a gasp, tiny freckles he hadn't noticed before dotting her nose beneath the tempting blush. Cupping her head in his hands, he lowered his lips to hers, and captured them in a passionate onslaught. A need to let her know she was his swept over him, and he groaned at the softness of her mouth, the feel of her tongue dancing against his as he ground his hips into her.

Ryder let his hands fall to her slim shoulders, his stomach flipping as she let out a moan at his touch, sliding them across her creamy skin. His groin tightened as he brushed his lips down her throat, pausing to nip gently at her earlobe as he let his hands skim lower. Palms cupping her curves, he let out a laden groan as she writhed against his body, sliding her hip up against his as her heel dug into his thigh, pulling him closer.

Glancing up for a moment, drugged with the passion that shone in her eyes, Ryder latched his hands onto the firm roundness of her bottom, hoisting her up into his hold as he held her hungry stare. "Elizabeth, I...I have to say something. When I thought I would never see you again—"

"Sh. It didn't happen," she responded in a throaty whisper that made him swallow anxiously, placing a trembling finger against his mouth. "It didn't happen."

"I know that, but listen. I didn't say something, and I want to say it now." Ryder passed his tongue nervously over his lips, his chest squeezing as he readied himself to say words that had never before left his thoughts. "I...I love you, you know. I do. I love you. And little Thomas too, even if I haven't had a chance to get to know him properly yet. He's adorable. I swear I'll watch over him forever, as though he was my own son. He was so brave down there in Helheim, trying to fight that Warder off and everything. I don't think I've ever been prouder of a little kid before. And you..." he trailed off, clawing his hands into her flesh as the burning need to sink himself inside her rose again. "You're incredible, and more than I deserve."

Elizabeth bent her torso to lean down to him, grasping his face in her hands as she gazed earnestly down at him. "Ryder, I love you too. And you deserve me. I deserve you. I don't know what happened to you before you were a reaper, but it doesn't matter." She wriggled against him, and Ryder's eyes half-closed at the movement, feeling the heat from under her skirt pressing into his body. "The man I've known since I met you is kind, generous, selfless and brave. Whatever you were...you're not him anymore. You're my Ryder now."

Her words slammed into him, and some hole, somewhere deep in his chest, was finally filled. Everything clicked together, the world around him coming into sharp focus as he studied her smiling face. Growling with lust, he bunched her skirt up into his fingers, still gripping her tightly against the wall. He bent his head to lather kisses along one pale, bared thigh resting against his arm, and glanced back up with a wry grin. "I'm your Ryder, forever. I promise. Now come and ride *me*."

Elizabeth purred in anticipation, her face breaking into a delighted smile. "I never thought you'd ask." Trailing a finger along the winding skull and fire tattoo peeping from under the sleeve of his jacket, she murmured, "I've been dying to see how far this tattoo leads."

EPILOGUE

Two Weeks Later

Sunlight shone brightly through the clean windows, casting a yellow glow over the piles of magazines and clothes rapidly being picked up by McKenna and Mika. Elizabeth stood back with a satisfied nod, looking up at the gleaming glass with the dripping sponge in her hand, her hair coiled up on her head in a knotted scarf. "There," she announced happily, "good as new. I bet they haven't looked that clean in years."

McKenna glanced up from her own work, blinking against the brilliance that shone through. "I'll say. We might need some curtains," she chuckled, returning the smile that Elizabeth sent her way.

Alisha flashed a grim expression at the three male reapers seated on the sofa, a duster in her hand, all of them staring over at the football game on the TV with unblinking eyes, scoffing, "You know, this would go a lot faster if you guys actually helped. Don't you care that you're sitting in your own filth?"

"Didn't bother you before," Devin retorted cheekily, dodging the cushion she threw at him with a laugh. "Besides, you ladies are doing such a good job. And our team's winning. This is important."

"Right," Elizabeth smirked, coming over to join Alisha Nudging the woman by her side, she added, "Would be a shame if we turned that TV off though."

"Aw, come on!" Ryder cried out, leaping up and skirting the sofa to wrap his arms around Elizabeth's waist. He planted a loud kiss on her lips, catching her up and swinging her around. "Let us have our 'boy's time'. We're doing all that male bonding and stuff. Aren't we, little fella'?" he added, putting her down and bending over the back of the sofa, ruffling Thomas' hair.

Thomas glanced up with a disarming grin, jumping up onto the seat and waving a piece of crayoned paper excitedly. "Yeah, male bonding, Mummy. With me and Ryder." Ryder smiled back at the little boy. In the two weeks Thomas and Elizabeth had been part of his life, he had never felt happier. Elizabeth was the woman he had never known he needed, and Thomas was the son he had never had. The boy was as irrepressible as he was cute, and not a day went by when Ryder didn't want to spend every waking hour with both of them. He had carried out two more collections since their arrival, and his heart felt lighter every time he could return to them and make sure they were safe, carrying Thomas on his shoulders and hugging Elizabeth close.

Thomas tugged on his sleeve, bringing him back into the present, waving the sheet of paper in his face urgently. "You have to look at this," he said solemnly, his little face serious as he pulled eagerly at Ryder's arm. "It's a picture for you."

"Aww, thanks, mate!" Ryder grinned, taking the offered piece of paper and casting his eyes over it. Thomas had drawn three stick figures together, underneath a rainbow and yellow sun. The smallest one was obviously Thomas, drawn with crayon and a wide smile, the stick figure's arms holding onto the arms of the other two. One of them had long yellow hair—obviously Elizabeth—and the other one had dark hair and a gun in his hand. All of them were smiling and stood together, as one.

Jumping up and down in a fit of glee, Thomas jabbed a finger into the stick figure with the gun. "See, that's you. And me, and Mummy. And you're protecting us. And we're all happy, in the sunshine." He glanced up at Ryder, his green eyes bright with waiting anticipation for approval.

Just when I thought I had no more heartstrings to be tugged, the kid does it again. Sucking in a deep breath, Ryder leaned down and kissed the top of Thomas' sandy hair, hugging the boy in close. Releasing him before he could be accused with a tiny finger and solemn expression how 'girly' he was being, he responded, "That's brilliant. Just brilliant, mate."

Contented that his artwork had brought the desired effect, Thomas smiled at Ryder and his mother before plumping back down onto the sofa, twisting around to watch the football once again with his new 'uncles'. Elizabeth gave Ryder a tight squeeze, bringing his attention back to her, and stood on her tiptoes to give him a peck on the nose. "He loves you to bits, you know."

Ryder chuckled, stroking his hand down her silky hair. "I'm pretty fond of the little guy, myself."

He released his hold on her as she went back over to the windows with Alisha, the two of them muttering and giggling, and he turned to look around with a deep frown. Clearing his throat, he asked loudly, "Where's Gabe? Shouldn't he be back by now?"

Drew broke his attention for a moment, glancing around the room. His eyebrows furrowed, and he gave a nod. "You're right, he should. He's been gone for hours. Not like him at all."

Thomas' eyes opened wide, and he cried out, "Where's Uncle Gabe? Is he okay?"

Realising their mistake of talking out loud, Drew and Ryder exchanged glances, Drew forcing a smile onto his face and patting Thomas affectionately on the arm. "Of course not. He's just a bit late. He'll be back soon, don't worry." As the small boy settled back into his seat, satisfied with the explanation for now, Drew rose up and skirted the sofa. Devin made as though to follow, but his twin shook his head and pointed towards Thomas. Understanding what he meant, Devin nodded gently and shuffled closer to Thomas, quickly distracting him with talk of football. Drew jerked his head towards the kitchen, and Ryder moved forwards with him, both of them rounding the corner and shutting the door behind them.

The noise muted from the TV in the other room, Ryder whispered, "What should we do?"

Drew gave a heavy sigh, shrugging his shoulders. "I don't know. I daren't say 'go look for him'. Not when it's better that we stay together as a unit." Shaking his head, Drew slammed his hand down onto the counter, leaving a mark in the dark grey surface. "From now on, we go out in pairs. Not alone."

"Agreed. But that doesn't help us right now," Ryder reminded him, searching his friend's worried face with a cool gaze. "Do we know where he went?"

Drew nodded, hope lighting up his face for a moment. "Yeah, he went over to some building on the west side of town. You know, where all those expensive old Victorian houses are? The 'rich' side of town."

"Good, at least we know." Ryder folded his arms over his chest, glancing up at the mounted clock on the wall. "I say we give it another hour, and if he's still not back, we go and look for him. We'll leave the others here."

Something was very wrong. Gabe could feel it in his blood. He slowly rounded the corner, clicking the safety off the gun in his hand. It might not do much against the tension rising in his body, but it made him feel safer. *Damn it. I shouldn't have come alone. None of us should be going out alone anymore.*

The place he had been drawn to was strange enough. Reapers were supposed to find souls to send back to the Hall, but the problem was that he couldn't find anyone to send. The house was deserted, a beautiful Victorian mansion, rotting from its core and decrepit with neglect. The windows downstairs were boarded over, and dust bunnies danced together in the thin streams of sunshine filtering onto the landing. The house creaked and groaned as though it was alive, and Gabe gave a shiver as the sounds sent an icy finger of fear along his spine.

His stomach twisted, and he snapped his attention to a door on the left. *Yes, that's the one.* Swallowing back his anxiety, Gabe stepped forwards boldly and made his way over. Reaching out a hand, he pressed his palm against the panelled wood and pushed gently. It creaked on its hinges as it swung open, wailing in protest as its aged form shuddered. His dark olive eyes roved around the interior of the bedroom, his pulse leaping under his skin. There was no one there. An array of antique furniture greeted him, a brass bed in the centre, surrounded by pink wallpaper and a little girl's toys. Dolls were arranged neatly on the pillow, their porcelain faces smiling coldly back at him as he edged inside, keeping a tight grip on his weapon. *Something is here. I can feel it.*

A tall, cream wardrobe separated him from the right-hand side of the room, and he crept over to it, glancing across its gilded patterns, carved into each side. Leaping around the heavy piece of furniture, he snapped his gun up in readiness, darting his eyes left and right, searching the room. *Nothing.* Relaxing, he lowered the gun and let out a soft sigh, rubbing the back of his neck as the hairs rose up. *Fuck it. I'm leaving. Whatever's here, it doesn't want to be found. I'll come back with one of the others, and —*

His thoughts were broken by a sound. Gabe listened intently, furrowing his brows in concentration. It sounded like the bubbling of water, but it was far away and distant, as though it was rushing deep in his ears. Glancing around, his attention was caught by a floor-length mirror at the far end, perched beside a dust-coated dollhouse. The colour drained from his face, and the hand holding the gun trembled in response to what he saw instead of his reflection.

The room was not reflected in the mirror's gleaming surface. The image rippled with water, trapped bubbles of air making their way up towards the unseen surface, light refracting into shards as it travelled through the deep blue. But the most chilling part of the scene was the figure. A young girl, her mouth opening and closing with silent words, floated in the centre of the mirror. Her long black hair floated in tendrils around her pale face, her bright blue eyes locked with Gabe's terrified gaze. He dropped to his knees at the sight, prickles sliding across his skin and freezing him in place.

It was his dead daughter.

The Grim Alliance Series

Reaper's Deliverance (Book 1)

Promises of the Dead (Book 2, coming 3rd September 2014)

A Cursed Life (Book 3, coming 5th November 2014)

ABOUT THE AUTHOR

I'm Miranda Stork, and I'm addicted. Addicted to writing and reading books, anyway. And chocolate, but that's another issue - no interventions, please.

I live in the middle of a forest in North Yorkshire, spending my spare time as the wild woman of the woods, scaring small children and upsetting the sheep. On the days that I feel like being civilized, or I haven't got any unicorns to ride, I sit down and pour the tumbling thoughts in my head out onto digital paper. Mainly the thoughts and characters come out in paranormal form, with a good smattering of romance, because everyone likes a good cuddle. But you can also find strong elements of thrillers, myths, and even dystopia amongst the pages of all my novels. I've wanted to write books ever since I first realised that fairytales were not the newspapers of the fairy kingdom, but the imaginings of actual people who wanted to tell fancy made-up stories to other people. From that moment, I was hooked.

Why do I write? Good question. It might be easier to just keep the stories in my head, or even just to write them for myself. But I want to share them. There is no greater delight for a writer than when a reader devours your book, and declares, "Something in that novel resonated with me. And I want MORE." So grab your lucky clover and a baseball bat (there's some nasty paranormal creatures where we're going), eat the cookie with 'eat me' tagged on it, and enter through the tiny door into the world of Miranda Stork...

Read more at www.moonrosepublishing.com!

Enjoyed this book from Moon Rose Publishing? Why not come check some more out at www.moonrosepublishing.com?

Bringing the impossible to life through our pages.